AN AVALON ROMANCE

THE MORE I SEE
Lisa Mondello

As a top-notch cutting horse trainer, Cody Gentry was riding high until he lost his eyesight after a freak chemical accident. Unable to see the hand in front of his face, never mind the horse or cattle he trained, he feels his life is over and slips deep into depression. His whole future hinges on the success of an eye surgery that could give him his old life back.

When guide dog trainer, Lyssa McElhannon, arrives on his ranch like Florence Nightingale coming to save him, he wants no part of her or her guide dog. But something about Lyssa's musical laugh coupled with her tenacity digs under his skin and won't let go.

Having been blind most of her life, Lyssa understands the paralyzing fear Cody feels after losing his vision. But she refuses to let the stubborn cowboy waste his life away sitting in a chair when she knows firsthand that a good guide dog can change his world. She just needs one month to prove it to him.

Falling in love with Cody was not part of Lyssa's plan, nor was having him open her eyes to see that there was a whole lot of living she'd been missing out on.

THE MORE
I SEE

•

Lisa Mondello

AVALON BOOKS
NEW YORK

PRINTED IN THE UNITED STATES OF AMERICA
ON ACID-FREE PAPER
BY HADDON CRAFTSMEN, BLOOMSBURG, PENNSYLVANIA

This book is dedicated with love to Melyssa, LeeAnne, Becky and Ben, my shining stars.

Acknowledgments

A special thanks to Diane Piazzo and Otis (the Wonder Dog), both of whom inspired me to write this book, to Punk Carter for teaching me the sport of cutting from afar and reading my chapters, to Amy Vohres of the National Cutting Horse Association and Michelle Lavitt of The Guide Dog Foundation for the Blind. Any mistakes in interpreting facts are the author's.

Chapter One

There was nothing extraordinary about Alyssandra Orchid McElhannon but her name. She was used to being invisible where men were concerned. Men were an unusual breed for sure. This one was no different.

Lowering her sunglasses, she blinked as she peered at the long, lean man stretched out on the lawn chair by the pool. So this was Cody Gentry. The man that insisted she come all the way from the Houston school where she'd worked to personally train him here on the Silverado Ranch.

At least Cody Gentry had a valid excuse not to notice her. He was blind.

He made no move to indicate he'd heard her approach, or the soft sound of dog claws scratching on the concrete as she led her guide dog closer. No tilt of his head, no lift of his long fingers, weaved tightly together on his lap, not even a twitch of his booted feet, crossed and slightly hanging over the end of the lawn chair.

Lyssa slid the sunglasses back up the bridge of her

1

nose. He could be asleep, she decided. By the slump of his shoulders and the angle of his head, cocked to one side, his white straw cowboy hat tilted over his face ever so slightly, it was certainly possible. It would explain why he'd yet to have even a slight reaction to her approach.

She knew how acute the other senses were when one was lost. She'd outfitted herself in her usual garb, a pair of well-worn blue jeans, a cool cotton button-down shirt, and a comfortable pair of sneakers. She could understand how the soft soles of her sneakers would be muffled. Lyssa wasn't the most graceful person, but she wasn't a clod. If Cody hadn't heard the sound of her footsteps, he should have at least noticed the telltale sound of Otis' paws on the walkway.

Maybe he wasn't asleep. Maybe he was just being rude. Mike Gentry, Cody's father, had warned as much.

It had been only a week ago that Mike Gentry first approached the Houston Guide Dog School asking for immediate help, insisting his son needed a one-on-one instructor. If only the school could send someone to the ranch, he said, it might break through the deep, impenetrable depression that had overtaken his son since a freak chemical accident had rendered him blind nearly eight months earlier. It might help him get back among the living again.

Lyssa had been in the office the day Mike Gentry strode in with deep pockets and endless arguments about why he needed someone immediately. The director had been insistent that the school offered only month-long classes to students who stayed on their campus. While what Mike was asking for his son was not unprecedented, it was usually reserved for extreme cases.

The money Mike offered to gift the school spoke of his desperation. Right in front of Lyssa, he'd offered what amounted to enough money to service several dogs to those in need. After a failed corneal transplant, the likelihood that Cody would get his eyesight back was slim to none. Cody needed to become functional again in his own environment, and without the aid of a guide dog, he wouldn't be able to get around.

Mike had assured the school that Cody was eager to work with a guide dog, but given life on the ranch, he felt that training should be conducted in the environment where the dog and handler would spend the bulk of their time.

Lyssa found she couldn't stay quiet. There was time before the next class started. She had a dog ready and, even with the limited information Mike Gentry had offered about his son, Lyssa felt the match might work.

Peering over at Cody now, she realized the depression Mike Gentry spoke of was much worse than he had let on.

The desperation, the depression. Lyssa had seen it happen before. Although, since she'd lost her own eyesight at such an early age, she didn't remember feeling it herself. When she regained her sight after twenty years of living in darkness it was cause for celebration. New miracle surgery—an option that wasn't open to everyone. Yet. But Lyssa was sure that one day it would be. The advances modern science had made astounded her.

Until that day came, she had the incredible task of

trying to pull this six-foot-plus man out of his despair by showing him that life was still worth living without his vision.

She sighed, noticing the heavy slump of his shoulders. She had her work cut out for her.

She commanded Otis to sit and the well-trained dog heeded the command instantly. Lyssa cleared her throat. The man didn't move.

As she suspected, he'd heard her perfectly well. He simply chose to ignore her.

"I was told I could find Cody Gentry out here by the pool," Lyssa finally said.

The muscles on his face twitched slightly. "Who's looking?"

The timbre of his voice was deep, with a faintly ominous edge that reminded Lyssa of the voices she'd heard as a child when she and Kim would sneak downstairs in the middle of the night and watch old horror flicks on cable. She couldn't see the movies, she'd only heard the voices. That added to the mystery, raised the level of anticipation, sending shivers racing up her spine.

Cody wasn't anything out of a horror movie. She ignored the swell of apprehension that had her confidence faltering.

She knew better than to extend her hand in a normal greeting for her introduction. Instead, she drew in a deep breath and hoped her voice sounded pleasant. "I'm Alyssandra McElhannon."

He didn't move. "What do you want?"

"I brought Otis," she said cheerfully.

"What's Otis?"

"Otis is a who, not a what."

His whole body seemed to stiffen. His voice was

controlled, but edgy enough to send shivers chasing over her skin. "I'm sorry you came all the way out here like this. Apparently someone failed to give you adequate information. I'm not training cuttin' horses anymore."

"Oh, Otis isn't a horse. He's a dog. Your guide dog. And I'm here to train the two of you to work as a team." She said the words with the pride she couldn't help but feel. Otis, like many dogs trained as seeing aids for the vision-impaired, was a lifeline to independence.

He sat still, unaffected. It wasn't at all the reaction she'd been expecting.

"Not interested."

"And you would be Cody Gentry, I take it?" she asked, already knowing he was.

"I just said I'm not interested."

"And I heard you. My job is to make you interested."

"Says who?"

Confused, she said, "Mike Gentry, for one."

He groaned audibly and straightened up in his chair. "My father sent you, huh?"

"That's right. He didn't tell you I was coming?"

"Did he already pay you for your troubles?"

"Well, yes, a portion is—"

"Then you're fired. I'll make sure you get the rest of the money you're owed by mail. I'm sorry he wasted your time."

Lyssa's huff was slightly exaggerated. Cody was as difficult as Mike Gentry had warned, but in a totally different way than Lyssa had been prepared for.

"In the first place, the school pays my salary and it is run entirely by donations. Second, training my dogs and students is never a waste of my time. Furthermore, you aren't the one who hired me, your father did. In fact, he asked me to stay on at the ranch until you and Otis were working well together. So, you can't fire me, no matter how much you squawk."

He made a face that almost made her laugh. "Squawk?"

Crossing her arms across her chest, she said, "I call it like I see it."

"Listen, Ms. McElfen—er—McEllaf . . . What's your name again?"

"McElhannon," she said slowly. "Alyssandra Orchid McElhannon. If we're going to be working together, I'd prefer to keep things informal. So you can call me Lyssa, if it's easier."

Easier and infuriating, she knew. Just because he couldn't see her, didn't mean he couldn't hear perfectly well. In fact, she knew his hearing was much better now than it had been before he'd lost his eyesight.

"Okay, Lyssa. I appreciate your crusade here, but you really are wasting your time. And mine, for that matter. I don't need a dog, and I don't need you. I need my eyes back. And if you can't give me that, then get out of my way! I don't want you or your dog here."

Anger flared so strong through her whole being that Lyssa could taste its bitterness. Part of Mike Gentry's argument that Cody needed a one-on-one instructor was because of his environment. He'd warned Cody could be difficult to work with, but explained he was there on Cody's behalf and that Cody was anxious to start training as soon as possible. He had attitude, but a strong desire. The only way to show Cody exactly how infuriating he could be was to throw it back in his face, his father had told her. Fight fire with fire. That seemed to be the only way to break through Cody's despair lately.

Lyssa couldn't argue with that. Cody had plenty of attitude. But Lyssa had underestimated the warning and now regretted it. Fight fire with fire? In her estimation, she was going to need to set off a case of C4 explosives to even make a dent.

"Otis and I aren't going anywhere," she said calmly. "At least not for the next month."

"A month?"

"That's right."

Anger simmered to a boil just beneath the surface of Cody's exterior, it seemed. His movements were quick and deliberate as he sat up straight and dropped his boots to the ground with a thud. She wanted to take a step back to shield herself from the slap of anger she was sure he was about to unleash, but she held her ground.

Lyssa had been too young to feel the anger when she'd lost her eyesight. She learned, just as a child learns to crawl and then walk, how to live in her dark world. Learning to crawl for a child was second nature. Curiosity won over confidence every time, hands down. Get from point A to point B and it didn't matter how you got there as long as you did it.

Learning to crawl as an adult, however, was utterly different.

Lyssa stayed rooted in her place and silently watched Cody stumble, disoriented, trying to rise from the lounge chair. He then felt his way around the table to the back of the chair. He lifted his head and an almost imperceptible sigh of relief escaped his lips. Cody dragged in a breath of air and began walking, his body tall and proud, his hands rooted at his side instead of out in front of him as a guide.

He must have memorized the amount of steps. Even in his stubbornness, his instinct for survival took over. Maybe she could use that to her advantage. Make it his. She wasn't going to give him an inch, though. She suspected a single step back for Cody would feel more like a mile.

Eight steps.

He didn't need her here. Not right at that moment. But she gave it one more try to see if she could make a small crack in his resolve.

"If you'd like, Otis will take you in."

He reached the door and lifted his hands, floating them out in front of him until they made purchase with the outer wall of the house. "I told you I don't need the dog."

"Yeah, I heard you. But counting eight steps only gets you from the chair to the house. What do you do when you're out in the fields? There aren't any chairs out there. Or is that some place you never venture anymore?"

His whole body became rigid. But he said nothing.

Lyssa shifted her weight to one hip and crossed her arms as she looked out into the green and gold pastures that rolled deep into the horizon.

"I suppose you could count the fence posts, or even paces to the fence, but turning around would be a bear. You could end up walking all the way to the county line before you hit the other side of the ranch."

"Your point?" he said haughtily.

"Otis can help you get around. Help you climb out of your eight steps and make it a hundred or more."

He dismissed her easily by turning and carefully walking through the French doors.

She released a slow breath, felt her shoulders sag slightly. Guilt should be gnawing at her insides by now for stripping down his reality, but she had no other choice. In her experience, it was either depression in a comfortable chair for the rest of his days, or it was living again. She was determined to make sure Cody Gentry chose right.

In the meantime, Lyssa had a few strong words for his father.

Where the heck was his father? And how dare he invite some snotty woman into the house to fix what couldn't be fixed, Cody fumed silently as he moved through the kitchen. A dog? What the heck was he thinking? Anyone with an ounce of sense or optical training knew that life as he knew it was over.

"Isadore, have you seen my father?" He knew the housekeeper was in. Ever since the accident nearly eight months ago, the petite woman, who'd been a regular fixture in the main house for as long as he could remember, had taken to keeping her eyes on him.

"He's not back from Houston yet," she said. He heard the scrape of a pan against the metal stovetop. He was sure the pot was empty and she was just trying to act busy, as she always did when he caught her watching. No doubt she was the one who'd told Lyssa McElfen, or whatever her name was, he was outside by the pool.

"He's with Ms. Waite."

Terrific. Dad's new lady friend. Cody supposed he should be happy for his old man, having been widowed for more than seven years now. His trips to Houston were becoming longer and more frequent.

"Has Beau made himself scarce, too?"

"Your brother is out with the horses, I think. He's been out a long while and should probably be in soon. Do you need me to get him?"

Cody sighed, a fingernail of irritation scratching its way to the surface of his composure. But he didn't bark out at Isadore. He knew better.

"No, don't bother. I'll find him."

The last thing he wanted was for Isadore to rush right out to find Beau. His relationship with his brother had been tenuous at best since Beau went on the road. He'd left home nine years ago to pursue fame on the rodeo circuit as a bronc bareback rider, leaving Cody a pile of ranch work and his dad's bad moods to deal with because of it. The World Championship title would have been his had he not come back to Texas and married the daughter of their father's biggest rival, opening up a rodeo school on the ranch his dad had always wanted for himself.

Thanks to the accident that took Cody's eyesight, his dear brother was now doing double duty back at the Silverado Ranch, stepping into Cody's boots as easily as if he'd never been gone.

"What do you know about our new guest?"

He sensed Isadore's hesitation in her hitch of breath. "Mr. Gentry asked me to get the guest bedroom ready. She is staying in the room next to yours."

"Ain't that convenient," he groaned, nearly under his breath.

Not quiet enough, however. Isadore's glare penetrated him, as harsh as the hot Texas sun. He didn't have to see the scowl on Isadore's face or the fist planted firmly on her aproned hip to know that was the picture in front of him now.

"You be polite to her. Ms. McElhannon seems like a very nice young girl."

"I'll be my usual charming self."

"Hmm, that's what I'm afraid of."

He fought the smile that pulled at his cheeks as he felt along the wall of the kitchen and down the hallway.

He had a good idea where Beau was at, but the arena was not a place he wanted to be right now. Not when his nerves were frazzled as if he'd been running a caffeine IV into his veins all day.

Twelve steps. He pushed through the front door. *Three steps.* He gripped the rail and eased himself down to the walkway. This was *his* ranch. He knew every inch of it, had committed it to memory long ago and could call up any image at will. He didn't need a stupid dog to help him get around.

The walkway led to the gravel driveway and beyond that, the field of high grass. He could almost see the tall blades bending against the light breeze, creating a ripple of green and gold in the sun. In the distance, he could hear a tractor, most likely mowing and scoring the piles of clippings to bake in the sun before being tied into bales.

Cody walked toward the sound, slowly, deliberately, noting the sudden change beneath his boots as he moved from gravel to grass.

"Where are you heading?" Beau called out from his left. His brother was still a good distance away.

"For a walk. You got a problem with that?"

"No, but you might when you end up in the pond you're heading towards."

Cody groaned as heat crept up his neck and seared his cheeks. "At least by then I'll know what direction I'm heading in."

"That's for sure. Do you—"

Beau was about to ask him if he needed anything. A simple question, Cody knew. He just hated hearing it from his big brother.

New wife, new baby, Beau seemed to have it all. And now he was here working Cody's horses and filling his size 12 boots with ease.

Cody supposed he should feel grateful. Although they never seemed to see eye to eye on just about anything, he trusted Beau like no one else. And yeah, his love for his brother ran deeper than the earth he was standing on, despite the bad feelings that had worked their way between them over the years. That was never going to change.

But right now, Beau's very presence on the ranch nagged at Cody like an annoying insect. He didn't want Beau's help. Didn't want anyone's help. He wanted to be able to get up in the morning and work like he'd done his whole life.

He couldn't see how his hands had changed over these last eight months, but he knew they had. He could feel it. The calluses, buried deep in every inch of his palms, had been there his whole life. A working man's hands. Now they'd grown soft from a lack of the physical labor that had dug those marks in deep. He fisted his hand and squeezed, trying to feel what was no longer there.

In the distance, Cody could hear an unfamiliar dog barking and the musical laugh of a woman. Not just any woman. Alyssandra Orchid McElfen or whatever.

The woman had a mouthful of a name to go with that sharp-edged attitude.

Still, as much as Cody wanted her gone, he couldn't help but wonder what the woman was like. How that sass in her voice translated to the way she walked or her looks. When she was angry, did she stand rigid, balling her fists at her hips?

Unlike the softness his hands had developed, a woman's touch was a softness he'd missed sorely these past months. And for all the steam Lyssa had spewed at him by the pool, Cody found himself wondering about the woman whose carefree laughter was floating to him from the distance.

There hadn't been an ounce of pity in Lyssa's voice, which to Cody was a welcome relief. If he heard one more worried syllable asking how he was getting along, he didn't think he could stand it.

He sighed as he sat on a section of freshly mowed grass and absentmindedly sifted through the stray clippings that were now baked bone-dry from the hot sun. It didn't matter what Lyssa and his father had cooked up for him. He didn't need a dog.

And he didn't want anyone's pity because his life was now dug deep in a hole. In a matter of weeks his eyes should be healed enough to try for another transplant. Despite what his old man thought, Cody hadn't given up. He was dealing with what life dealt him. His own way.

Lyssa was right about one thing, he realized as he sat there in the hot sun. Something as simple as walking across the yard, the same yard that had been his playground as a child, had become a dangerous affair.

Early on, when Cody had refused to believe the doctor's assessment that his eyes were shot, Cody had surged on. He was a worker from the cradle. Hands in dirt, feet in muck, and he didn't care. Nothing was ever going to keep him down, never mind a simple chemical accident.

It was just stupid drain cleaner that had landed him where he was. It wasn't as if the ranch hadn't had other young hands that were wet behind the ears and stupid in the ways of basic safety. It had been sheer bad luck that had him in the crossfire when the chemical cocktail the impatient ranch hand had mixed exploded. It was also Cody's fast action that had prevented that young hand from getting killed.

Tossing a handful of blades to the ground, he chuckled wryly at the irony. At one time Isadore had said he had eyes like a hawk, seeing every little detail that happened on this ranch no matter where he was standing. Every acre was etched in his memory. He knew every swell of green pasture, every upturned stone that built the natural fences along the property, as if Mother Nature herself had laid them that way on purpose. He closed his eyes and imagined it as it had been the last time he'd sat by the pond and looked out at the ranch he knew so well.

The Silverado Ranch had always been his home, and his childhood memories, plentiful and lush, only dug his roots in deeper, and made the love for this land that much stronger. It was lost to him now. But the memories were there.

They'd been a trio as kids, him, Beau and Jackson, running through the fields when their old man had relieved them of their daily chores. Brock was too young to keep up with them, the gap in years too wide from the older three boys. Too young to share in the trouble young boys usually met up with when exploring. And they hadn't really wanted him tagging along. Not then, anyway.

It was one of Cody's deepest regrets now. In times of crisis, he could count on his brothers. But the space in age between Brock and the rest of the Gentry boys had left the youngest boy on his own more times than not.

In the beginning, it was always the three of them, tamping down hay fields, running tracks in the high grass as they played cowboys and Indians. It had been a daily event, dashing through the vast playground that was theirs. Something as simple as finding the skeleton of a cow was like the biggest archeological find to three young boys out on an exploration. Bringing that find home to show their dad had their chests puffed out with pride.

Back then, their dad was just their dad. A cowboy from the cradle like his old man, and his before him. He used to say the land owned him, not the other way around.

But that had changed when Hank Promise moved in and bought the property now known as the Double T Ranch. The father Cody had known and loved had changed. And it had changed them all. Nothing ever felt the same again.

But what used to be was now all stored in his mind in a vivid spectrum of color. Now all he saw when he opened his eyes was a cold blackness.

The dog was getting closer, Cody realized with uneasiness. The prance of running paws on the ground grew louder and louder still until he could hear the dog panting. What was the dog's name again?

Before he could gather himself up and stand, the dog was by his side, licking his face.

"Knock it off," he groused, pushing the dog away with one hand while trying to stand. Despite his attempt to keep it back, a smile tugged at his lips.

"Otis, heel," Lyssa commanded, still from a comfortable distance. That little bit of time allowed Cody to stand up on his own without having to deal with the awkwardness of declining help.

The dog was still by his side, panting.

"Your name is Otis, huh?" He reached out and immediately the dog nuzzled his face to Cody's palm, allowing him to scratch behind his ears. He bent his head to get closer to the dog and whispered, "Don't get too used to this. I'm really a mean old bugger," he said with a slight chuckle.

Otis barked and Cody laughed.

In truth, he'd always loved dogs, all animals really. Something about what this dog represented gnawed at him though. It wasn't the dog's fault.

"Score one for Otis. You two look like best buddies already."

He heard the smile of satisfaction in Lyssa's voice and he snatched his hand away.

"Don't you keep your dog on a leash?"

She was out of breath, Cody realized, as if she'd run a mile. And with that image, he pictured the rise and fall of her chest as she took in air.

It wasn't good for him to think about Alyssandra McElfen, or whatever her name was, as a woman. The scent of her drifted to him on a slight gust of wind. A hint of vanilla mixed in with the sun-baked grass and dirt and gave Cody a heady feeling he wanted to shake off.

"Actually, I only keep him on his leash when he's in training, so he knows he's working. When he can roam free and exercise I let him. He's a working dog, but he's still a dog."

Otis was back for more affection and Cody obliged before he could think otherwise.

"He's tall. What breed is he?"

"German Shepherd. Most guide dogs are retrievers because their temperament is good and consistent. But we use shepherds, too. He's beautiful, not just his color and stand, but his personality. He's such a sweet thing."

"Now where have I heard that before?"

She chuckled and Cody had the amazing image of Lyssa's nose crinkling just slightly, the mental image of it making his head swim. He wondered how true that was.

"Don't let him scare you off," Beau called out. This time the sound of his voice was closer than it had been before he'd sat down. Terrific. Now he had to deal with his brother too.

"She's the one that brought the beast," Cody said sarcastically.

"I was talking about you and you know it." He could tell Beau had turned toward Lyssa by the change in his voice.

"Cody's been an ornery old goat since the day he was born. Never forgave Doc Masterson for swatting his behind. But we keep him around for laughs."

"At least I'm not ugly."

"Says you," Beau shot back.

"Did you have anything to do with this?"

"Lyssa? Heck no, that was all Dad's doing, but I'm glad he did. It'll be nice having some female company on the ranch again."

The smile in Beau's voice was like fingernails to a chalkboard.

"Mandy ought to appreciate that."

"Mandy is the one who introduced us. She picked Lyssa up from the airport."

"Your wife is very nice," she said, the smile in her voice so obvious that it had Cody gritting his teeth. She hadn't talked to him that way.

"Great, so everyone knows everyone now. Everyone likes everyone. Now I can leave."

Beau's sigh was more of a grunt. "Well, if it were my choice I'd haul you out to the back of the barn and beat you with a board like an old rug just for your rudeness. We were raised better than to treat our guest with so little hospitality."

"I learned from you."

"Hey, you were still getting your dirty diaper changed when I was standing up by the—"

"Enough already!"

No one answered and Cody took the few seconds of silence to calm himself.

"Sorry about that, ma'am," Beau finally said, quietly.

"Lyssa," she corrected, her voice soft and sweet as summer rain. It irked Cody to no end how the smoothness of her voice changed when talking to Beau. With him, she'd been sharp, her voice holding little of the warmth he heard now.

He supposed he deserved it. No, he *had* deserved it. He'd been a horse's behind earlier. Had he been this ill-mannered with company as a child he probably *would* have been hauled out behind the barn for a whippin' by his old man.

Cody turned to leave, and a wave of panic smacked

him square in the chest. His head began to swim when he realized he had nothing to hold on to, nothing to ground him but the vast earth beneath his feet. Somehow in the commotion of the dog, the conversation, he'd gotten himself turned around and now had no idea which direction to take back to the house.

He hated it. Hated the helplessness consuming him. Hated even more that now he was forced to swallow a baseball-sized lump of pride and ask for help.

"I need to finish up with Sweet Sassy's Smile before I can get back to the Double T. Maybe you can talk this old bag into showing you around, Lyssa. It was nice meeting you."

"Likewise."

To Cody, Beau said, "Sassy's coming along real nice. You ought to think about coming out to see her. I can't imagine why but I think she misses you."

Cody's heart squeezed. Sweet Sassy's Smile, his four-year-old cutting horse, was his pride and joy. For two years he'd been training her every day. That is, until the accident. He'd never felt more connected to any living creature as he did when he was riding her, whether in the arena or out in the fields. It had been a long time. Too long. It hurt too much.

"You think about it." Cody could hear Beau's wide strides move along the grass, then hit the dry dirt as he walked away.

A cold ache settled inside him. He shouldn't be at war with his brother. The things they'd argued about as kids didn't matter now, and maybe they never had. But to hear Beau talking about Sassy, knowing he was enjoying the very thing that had driven Cody his whole life, tore into his soul.

Now Beau was gone and he was alone with Lyssa,

the savior his father brought to the ranch to exorcise the demons from his son's soul. Or at least get him a little further than from the house to the pool.

A gust of breeze kicked up some dust and blew it his way. He had no choice, Cody realized. Asking Lyssa for help now would be like saying yes to this ridiculous plan they all had to bring him out into the world again.

Just get it over with, he told himself sharply. He could lock himself in his room later if he wanted. Until then he could handle this much humiliation.

Before he could push the words past the prideful lump in his throat, Lyssa said, "I need to unpack my things and put out a bowl of water for Otis. If you don't mind, I would appreciate you showing me to my room."

He would have sighed with relief if he didn't catch himself. "Showing" Lyssa to her room would be easy as long as he kept up conversation and followed *her* to the house.

Maybe she knew that or sensed his panic. If his father had hired her, she must have been working with the blind for some time and knew he was standing there practically wetting his pants with fear. She was a smart woman for handling him when he didn't want to be handled at all and for that, a smile crept up inside him.

"After you," he said smoothly. And thank God, he couldn't see her smug smile.

Chapter Two

*N*ot *again.*

Lyssa groaned as she let the sheer curtains float back into place, unable to stand seeing Cody stretched out on that lawn chair by the pool one more second.

It was common for people to sink into depression after losing some function of their life, but for Cody Gentry, that had been allowed to go on far too long.

To start as a team, both Cody and Otis needed to be willing. Cody hadn't gotten there yet. *Not by a long shot.*

In the three long days since she'd arrived at the ranch, Lyssa had seen Cody very little except for his daily jaunt out to the pool. He kept to himself in his room mostly. Any coaxing on her part only made him withdraw deeper.

From what Beau had told him, Cody had become a bit unreachable. The stubbornness and determination that had made him a hardworking man his whole life was now the demon that chained him down.

He didn't want to move on. His whole life hinged

21

on the success of future surgery. Until then, he was in limbo.

Lyssa had to change all that. Having Mike Gentry away for the next month didn't help either. The owner and patriarch of the Silverado Ranch had left her stranded with no direction to reach the very person he'd hired her to teach. Moreover, he'd lied about Cody's willingness to participate. And then he'd left Lyssa to deal with that lie on her own.

Well, she'd deal with it all right, with some strong words to Mike Gentry as soon as she could reach him.

She slipped the leash on Otis and stroked him behind the ears the way she knew he liked it. If circumstances were different, she would have packed her bags that first day and taken Otis with her. She was certainly free to leave, but because of the agreement made between Mike Gentry and the school Otis was not.

Most of the guide dogs Lyssa trained were owned by the school, and the school continued to hold ownership even when they were placed with a handler. When a blind person no longer needed the services of their guide dog, the dog was returned to the school and placed with another handler. Extensive training went into each dog and their ability to act as guide to their handler was too invaluable to waste.

However, there were cases where a handler chose to retain ownership of a dog, which, on Mike Gentry's insistence, was the case with Otis. If Lyssa left the ranch now, she would have to leave Otis behind. All his skills, all his training would be wasted on a man who wanted nothing to do with him.

That simply wasn't an option for Lyssa.

It wasn't going to be easy for Cody. It never was when you had to try to redefine yourself.

Yeah, she'd gone through that herself when she'd regained her eyesight. What to do? So many things were now open to her when she could finally see the world in front of her face.

Kim had just graduated high school and was ready to go off to college when Lyssa finished college and started training at the school as an apprentice. Her younger sister had been her best friend. She had other friends, sure, but there was no one like her sister. And soon after she'd finally been able to see her sister's bright smile, she'd left for college.

For three years after she'd regained her sight, Lyssa dedicated herself to the very thing that had given her independence as a child. She was finally certified as a guide dog trainer. Any other profession just didn't seem right.

She was comfortable among the dogs, working with them, training them. And yes, she was always a little sad when it was time to say goodbye. It was impossible for her to keep her love from these animals she trained. Knowing the gift these dogs gave their new owners was enough to dry her tears.

This time it would be no different. But only if she knew Otis was doing what he was meant to do.

"Come on, Otis. Time to get started."

She held on to the leash with her left hand and let Otis guide her through the house. It was important for him to become familiar with his new surroundings. It was even more important for Cody to step in and take the leash himself. She needed to wean Otis off her as soon as possible if this transfer was to be successful.

But first, she had to convince one stubborn mule to

cooperate. How she was going to manage that, she
didn't have a clue.

Cody sat by the pool and listened. And listened.
And the fact that he knew he was listening for a bark
or the sound of Lyssa's voice irritated him. He
shouldn't care, but he knew he did. As much as he'd
tried to avoid her these last few days, the woman had
the uncanny ability to get under his skin, surprising
him when he least expected it.

He couldn't hear anything but a determined group
of hornets, most likely working at building a hive under the soffet. He made a mental note to talk to the
ranch foreman later about having it removed.

Crossing one boot over the other, he decided he
wouldn't give Lyssa the chance to catch him off guard
today. He'd been fine these last months without her
presence on the ranch. He'd get along just fine when
she finally gave up her crusade and left him alone to
deal with his life his own way.

Funny how the thought of that didn't leave him feeling as good as he'd once thought it would.

Cody was still at the pool when she made her way
downstairs. Good Lord, his fear had to be higher than
his boredom threshold.

Lyssa decided to take the long way around, getting
Otis familiar with the house by taking him out the
front door and going along the walkway to the back
where Cody was sitting.

"The sun's kinda hot out today. You ought to think
about putting some sunscreen on your face," she said,
taking the chair on the opposite side of the heavy
wrought iron table. She settled Otis next to her and

pulled the sunscreen out of her pack, putting the pack on the table.

The sun was tearing down hard, though it seemed a bit cooler than it had been in days. Still, with her fair skin, Lyssa knew the temperature could easily fool her into getting a nice burn.

"I have my hat on," he groused.

"So much for small talk."

"If you consider sunscreen small talk."

"Your father told me your face wasn't that badly burned in the accident."

"That's right. No ugly scars to frighten people away."

"All I meant is that the new skin still needs to be protected."

She scrutinized his face for a second. He still wore a dark pair of sunglasses, hiding his eyes. But even with them, she could see Cody was a handsome man when he didn't scowl. Okay, even *with* that undeviating frown he was still handsome, with his angular jaw and rough outdoorsy good looks.

"I'm never out here long enough these days to do any damage."

She sighed nonchalantly. "Then you're lucky. Me, I burn like a lobster even in fifteen minutes of direct sunlight. My skin is way too light to handle this Texas sun."

"Get a hat," he said, his lips lifting on one side in a lopsided grin.

She chuckled. He was trying way too hard to be difficult, and she suspected part of him was having some fun poking at her, even if he wouldn't admit it.

"I don't need a hat. Not like you cowboys do anyway. I spend a lot of time training the dogs outside, but I'm not out in the fields in direct sun for long periods of time like you are."

His sunglasses protected his eyes and hid the scarring, the marbleization that most likely occurred as a result of the chemical burn. She'd seen enough burn victims to know how truly awful it could be.

"How did it happen?" she asked. Immediately, his body tensed. "We don't have to talk about it if it's too painful."

Cody's voice was low when he finally spoke. "We had a young ranch hand who got a little impatient and decided to mix a nasty cocktail of chemicals to unclog a drain. I came along just as he was done mixing his potion."

She closed her eyes imagining the horrible scene in her mind. Lye burns were devastating. "Was he hurt badly?"

Cody bit his lip. "No. I pushed him out of the way and got the brunt of it myself."

A peculiar warmth enveloped Lyssa, making her smile. "You saved him."

"Some would see it that way."

She chuckled at his modesty. "You're a hero, Cody. He could have been killed mixing drain cleaners that way."

He averted his head, his expression closed off from her. "He learned a good lesson he's not likely to forget."

In the short time she'd known Cody, she'd already surmised he wasn't a man who spoke big about his accomplishments. He wasn't someone who needed affirmation that he'd done well. He just did what had to be done.

Admiration for what he'd done filled her anyway as

she leaned forward in the chair, resting her elbows on her bare thighs. The skin on skin contact felt sticky.

"Why don't we get real daring and move beyond talk about sunscreen and accidents . . . oh, I don't know, go for a walk. Otis and I have been getting acquainted with the area. You could show me around the stables and tell me all about your horses. What was the name of the one Beau was training—"

"I'm not in the mood."

She nibbled on her lip. "Look, I know how scary it can be."

"Do you?"

"Yes, I've been there."

"I'm sure you have. I'll just bet you've met lots of useless men like me who can't even find the bathroom stall unless they're taken by hand like a two-year-old."

She changed her voice, knowing beyond the harsh edge of Cody's voice lay a lot of fear. And she did know that fear too well. "I've helped a lot of people move beyond anger and frustration to a better life."

"Great, then you've earned a nice big gold star and automatic entry into heaven for being a hero."

"I'm not a hero, Cody. But you can be. To yourself. By getting out of that chair."

Lyssa's voice rose higher than she'd intended it to. And she realized for the first time since she'd arrived at the ranch that she was becoming desperate herself. Desperate that she'd fail.

He laughed wryly. "Sorry, Alyssandra, but you won't be finding a hero in a man who can't even cut his steak without some help."

Lyssa flinched. What nagged at her more than Cody's attitude was the fact that there was more than a grain of truth in his words. No, not the hero part.

She knew if Cody just opened himself up to the idea of how Otis could change his life, he *would* be a hero to himself and regain his independence. That is, if the rest of the family would stop treating him like that two-year-old he constantly complained about being.

Last night, she'd sat down at the dinner table and watched him with frustration as he tried to cut the steak they'd had for their meal. If Cody had gone to some classes for the blind, he would have learned how to deal with these things, gotten to a point where he felt comfortable asking for help if he needed it. Instead, he'd fumbled with his knife and fork only to have a slab of steak fall off the plate and onto the clean white linen tablecloth.

Nothing was said, but Isadore immediate brought him another dish with a fresh piece of steak, this time cut into smaller pieces for him.

It had to have been humiliating. But Cody never uttered a word. He didn't have to. He just didn't eat.

Lyssa suspected part of Cody's problem wasn't Cody at all, but the way those around him treated him. Maybe Mike Gentry's disappearance on the ranch had nothing to do with him lying to the school, as Lyssa had suspected, but with being unable to watch his son falter.

Regardless of the reason, Lyssa wouldn't contribute to it. She'd quietly speak to Isadore and the rest of the family to make sure they understood that as of right now, they had to treat Cody as a man who could stand on his own two feet. Because that was exactly what he was, even if he didn't believe it.

She stood. "I'm tired of sitting around. Let's go for a walk, Cody."

"I told you I'm not in the mood."

"Then get in the mood. Anything is better than wasting away by the pool. You've got your whole life ahead of you. I'm getting bored with this game of yours and no matter what you say I know you are, too."

"I apologize if I haven't shown you proper hospitality," he said, his voice dripping with sarcasm.

"Hospitality has nothing to do with it. You're being a coward."

"Get away from me," he said, his voice lethal, causing her to inch back in her seat.

She'd meant to get a charge out of him. Fight fire with fire. But instead, he seemed resigned with the fact that he was indeed a coward.

Heroes weren't only strong, able-bodied people who could leap tall buildings with a single bound. They were everyday, flawed people who yelled at their kids and cried with a friend. People who made mistakes, got shoved down and stood right back up. People who did the impossible when it seemed impossible. Not because they weren't afraid, but because they didn't have it in them not to act even when they were afraid.

Cody was that kind of hero. Lyssa could see it in him, even if he couldn't. She only had to listen to the stories from the people who worked on the ranch, hear the admiration for Cody in their voices, through their words, to know how much respect they all had for him. Cody just needed something to break him free from the anchor holding him down, something to show him that he could indeed be a hero and reclaim his life again. He needed a push.

Her pushes weren't even making him sway.

Lyssa turned away from the forlorn look on his face and immediately shielded her eyes from the sun's stinging glare on the surface of the pool water. Her skin was hot and it was only a matter of time before it would turn pink.

She wouldn't sit there, and she refused to allow Cody one more minute wallowing in self-pity. Pushing up the sleeves of her shirt in a huff, she said, "I'll be more than happy to get away from you, Cody. But just answer me this. What ever happened to getting back on that horse when you've been bucked off? Huh?"

"I fail to see how you can compare losing my eyesight with riding a horse."

Not allowing her frustration to get the better of her, she began to pace to clear her head before she spoke.

"It's the same thing. You've been thrown. I'll even give you that it was one heck of a fall. But the only logical thing to do is get up and go on."

"Go for your walk, Lyssa," he said coolly.

Her blood pounded in her head until she swore it would explode. The man was infuriating! She didn't care how depressed he was. He wouldn't even give it a try.

She swung away from him, bunching her fists up to her side, needing to gather up her irritation and seal it tightly in a bottle before she could try to calmly reason with him.

Blinded by frustration, she didn't calculate how close she was to the edge of the pool. With one step too many her bunched fists became outstretched wings as she tried to catch her balance. But it was too late, she was already going airborne. She took a deep breath before she plunged into the clear water.

"Lyssa?" Cody sat in silence, almost relieved. No, he was irritated as all get out. He'd been waiting for her, much as he hadn't wanted to. He'd pushed her away and now that she'd taken off, he . . . didn't really want her gone. What was it about this woman that had him seesawing back and forth?

Otis began barking and there was a scrape of paws on the concrete. Not only did the barking continue, but Otis had now added a frantic whine to it. He'd yet to hear the animal react so insistently.

Cody sat up straight and tried to hear above the dog's cries.

"Hey, Lyssa," he called aloud. "You forgot your dog!"

He wanted to be irritated that she'd gone off all half-cocked and left him with a barking dog but . . .

Splashing. Yes, there had been a splash. A choke, maybe a cough. He wasn't sure.

"Lyssa?"

There was another swoosh of water and his heart leaped to his throat, then started jackhammering in his chest.

"Lyssa, this isn't funny. Answer me," he said, his voice rising to a fevered pitch.

The dog continued to bark. Through the splashing, he heard nothing. No voices. No cry for help.

Where the heck was Isadore? She was always watching him. If something had happened she would have flown through the door by now.

He inched his way out of the chair with great control, easing himself over to where he thought the table was. But as he feared, with every wave of his hand, he couldn't connect with it. He listened, but only heard the dog's bark.

"What is it, boy? Did she leave without you? Did she fall in the pool?"

Another splash and a cold chill raced through him, making him shiver.

"Lyssa? Talk to me."

He dropped to his hands and knees and quickly moved away from the sound of the dog. He knew where the table was positioned in relation to the pool and the house, but somehow, maybe his chair had been moved and now his bearings were shot. God, he hated not being able to see!

He couldn't recall if he'd heard more than just a splash. Had she dove into the water? Maybe hit her head? He hadn't been paying attention. He'd been too angry. Too self-absorbed.

He closed his eyes as fear pummeled him, opening them again to the cold blackness that was always startling.

"Say something, Lyssa!"

Cody squashed down the hysteria filling him. If she'd fallen in the pool and hit her head somehow, it would be too late if he went in search of Isadore or Beau now. Brock wasn't home. He'd left earlier that morning and probably wouldn't be home until late.

He was already wasting too much time just thinking. Fear bubbled up his throat as he crept along the concrete, choking him. Pebbles dug into his palms and bit into his knees through his blue jeans as he crawled along the patio, feeling his way to the smooth edge of the pool. Otis was clearly upset by the splashing and that could only mean one thing. *Lyssa was in trouble.*

Holding the edge, Cody eased into the pool, felt the cool wetness seep into his clothes and chill his skin. All the while he was straining to hear which direction the splashes were coming from above the dog's bark. He could barely breathe, his heart lodged in his throat.

He tossed his hat and his sunglasses to the side of the pool, hearing the glasses connect with the concrete. He waded in waist deep toward the sound of the now occasional splash, until he reached a point where the pool's floor dipped.

"Lyssa?" he said. She wasn't answering and that wasn't a good sign.

The dog barked, and he heard the splash of water that may have been his own. He wasn't sure. Fear leveled him. Good God Almighty, how on earth would he find her?

He was a strong swimmer, had always been since he was a child. If he moved too quickly and she sank below him he might miss her. Deliberately, he forced himself to remain calm and move evenly. He dipped underwater, frustrated that he couldn't see any better below the water than he could above. As irrational as it seemed, the darkness still shocked him.

He concentrated on the sound happening underwater and pushed himself forward, arms moving back and forth. He heard a cough and came up for air, listened, then dove under again with another forceful thrust. He couldn't hear the splashing anymore.

"Lyssa," he called out when he came back up for air. He was in deep water, unable to touch the bottom. He hoped to God Lyssa wasn't below him. He moved again and felt his foot kick against something. Twisting his body around, he reached out and felt her arm, grabbing it as she lashed at him.

He drew her to him, feeling his way to push the hair from her face and her mouth. She coughed and with that sound relief flooded him. She might have swallowed water, but at least she was breathing. Her arms were thrashing, striking him in the face and shoulders, as if she were struggling.

"You're okay, Lyssa. I've got you," Cody said, hooking his arm around her and swimming in the rescue position that he'd learned years ago as a young boy taking lessons.

Lyssa was tinier than he'd imagined. The thought struck Cody hard, in contrast to his first impression of her. Although he had to admit he'd tried real hard not to imagine what Lyssa McElhannon was like behind all that sass and steam. And although she was a little bony, she was soft against him.

He pushed those wayward thoughts away and concentrated on his movement, on getting them both out of the pool.

His hand touched the edge of the pool and he felt his feet hit bottom. Relief washed over him as he stood and realized he was in the shallow end of the pool.

"Don't fight me. I have you. I won't let you go under," Cody said as Lyssa coughed. He picked her up and lifted her out of the water.

She coughed a few more times. "I'm okay. You can let go of me."

"Let me be the judge of that."

"I am. Please put me down."

He dropped the arm that held tight to her knees and felt the swish of water around his denim-clad legs as her feet submerged, but he held tight with his other arm around her waist. His boots, which he'd neglected to pull off in exchange for precious time, were now filled with water and made it difficult to move steadily.

"I'll help you climb out."

"No, really. I can do it. I just wasn't looking. I can't believe I fell in."

"I'm going to have Isadore call 911. You need to be checked."

"You're making too much of this. I'm fine. It was a simple accident."

"For God's sake, you nearly drowned, Lyssa. I just want to make sure you didn't swallow too much water."

"Please, Cody, I fell in the pool. Big deal. It's not like it's the first time I've done something this stupid."

"You mean, you make a habit of this sort of thing? Didn't you ever take swimming lessons?"

He felt droplets of water spray him as she shook her head. "No, I didn't. And I'm just not a good swimmer. I'm not very coordinated, either, it seems. Never been."

When they reached the stairs she climbed out first. He gripped the rail and climbed out behind her. Instinctively, he returned his arm to her waist without a thought of how he was going to get back to the house.

The dining room screen door opened and he heard the click of Isadore's shoes on the concrete by the pool.

"I turn my back for a minute to do laundry and you decided to take a swim without even changing into a bathing suit," she said, thrusting a terry towel in his hand.

He unfolded it and since he knew Lyssa was standing just next to him, he draped it around her shoulders and began to rub her back.

"I have a towel, thank you." Lyssa's voice was more breathless than it had been in the pool, and Cody started to worry that maybe she just didn't want to burden anyone.

"Isadore, please call the doctor. I want to make sure Ms. McElfen—"

"McElhannon," Lyssa quickly corrected.

"Lyssa fell in the pool and I want to make sure she wasn't hurt."

Isadore gasped. "My goodness, child, are you all right?"

Lyssa groaned. "You're both making way too much of this."

"Am I?" Cody asked.

He heard her soft sigh and wished he could see her face. He wished even more that she was in his arms so he could know that she was all right.

"Yes. Isadore, please don't call anyone. Please. I'd rather forget this happened."

Cody felt the dog's tail whip against his leg as he passed. Otis's barking and whining had stopped now that Lyssa was out of the pool. With a whoosh of air, Lyssa moved by him.

"You were so upset," Lyssa crooned to Otis. "You're such a good dog for alerting Cody that I fell in the pool."

Confusion filled him. "What are you talking about?"

"Otis alerted you by barking. Isn't that why you came in after me?"

"Yes, but . . ." he said, trying to keep his sudden skepticism at bay. "Is he trained to do that?"

"Well, no. He was resting by the table, not guiding me. It's hard to tell how any dog will react in a situation like this."

Irritation mingled with anger, simmering just below the surface of his composure.

"Otis alerted me," he said flatly.

She chuckled softly. "Well, yes. How else would you have known I fell in?"

"The big splash you made was a good clue," Cody said shortly.

"But he kept barking," Lyssa protested.

"And barking."

Lyssa hesitated, her voice a little unsure. "Yes."

"Tell me, how long did it take you to cook up this little scheme?"

She fell silent for a moment. "Cody, what on earth are you talking about?"

"You were the one who was talking about heroes. You tell me."

"I'm not sure I understand what you're getting at."

"I think you do. You wanted me to be a hero. Now you've done it. I've saved the day."

She laughed wryly. "I fell into the pool, Cody. You came in after me. I guess, yeah, that makes you my hero."

"And if I hadn't been here, what would have happened?"

She was silent.

"Don't you dare back down on me now, Lyssa. What would you have done?"

"I probably would have very ungracefully made my way to the side of the pool, climbed out, wrung out my clothes and felt pretty embarrassed about the puddles I'd made through the house."

He sighed, humiliation flaring up inside him. He was beginning to think Lyssa was different. What had made him think she'd see him as a man when no one else seemed to?

"Thank you for at least being honest."

"About what? Falling in the pool?"

"About staging this little—"

By the swoosh of air that belted him, he knew she'd swung around quickly. "Hey, wait just a second. I fell in the pool. Maybe I don't like admitting I can be a klutz, but that's the truth."

"You mean you didn't pretend to be drowning, either?"

"What are you talking about?"

He laughed, but the anger that had been simmering began to burn deep inside his gut.

"Is that part of your schooling, humiliating your students?"

"If anyone should be humiliated, it's me. I was angry and wasn't watching where I was going. I can't swim very well and I fell in the deep end of the pool. I'd swallowed some water and started coughing. I panicked. Before I knew what was happening you were wading into the pool after me. I didn't stage anything."

"No, you just stayed nice and quiet until I found you. Made me think you were in trouble so I could rescue you."

"No, that's not it at all. I wasn't drowning. But it would have taken me a while to get out of the pool on my own and I appreciate your help. Obviously you don't believe that so you can go ahead and think what you want."

"You lied."

"How do you figure that?"

"You pretended something that wasn't real."

She sighed heavily. "What's real is you got out of that chair and came in after me."

His laugh was harsh and his mouth tasted bitter. "Well, Alyssandra, you got me out of the chair, all right. Now, if you'll excuse me . . ."

"No. No more. You're not going to sink back into that hole after coming this far."

"Who gave you the right to come here and decide what hole I should or shouldn't be in? I don't want you here in my house or in my life. And I don't want your pity. Just take your dog and get out!"

"I can't! If I leave, Otis has to stay."

Ironically, his fury was blinding and he would have laughed if he didn't feel so darned lousy. His head pounded so strong it felt ready to explode.

"I don't want your dog."

"He's not my dog. Technically, he belongs to your father. So neither one of us has a say in this. And I won't let all his training go to waste because you're being so bull-headed."

Drops of water sprayed him, as if she'd turned to walk away, then swung back toward him quickly.

"Just for the record, there's nothing about you to pity. You're an able-bodied man who needed a kick in the butt and you're just sore that I, unwittingly, was the one to give it to you."

"I was doing perfectly fine before you showed up."

"Not from where I've been sitting!"

She turned and stomped toward where Otis was patiently waiting. She grabbed the leash and gave the forward command. With a scratch of claws on the ground, Otis immediately stood and began walking away toward the French doors. Cody heard the squeak of the patio door.

"Where are you going? I'm not done."

"Well, I am, and if you want to continue taking your bitterness out on me, you're going to have to come find me. I'm not putting up with you or your bad moods anymore. You're on your own."

"Wait a minute."

He didn't hear anything more except the quick slamming of the door.

"Lyssa!" he hollered, not caring that he was now inside the house and in his anger his voice was booming against the walls.

His boots were still filled with water, adding a burden to his movement that only fueled his anger. He yanked them off and tossed them aside. However, the puddles he'd created by dumping his boots, combined with his wet feet slipping on the slick surface of the floor, didn't make walking any easier.

Cody held his arms out straight and waved them back and forth, reaching for things he knew were there but couldn't see. His hip collided with a chair and then a table. He felt the centerpiece that had been filled with ceramic fruit for as long as he could remember tip over. The fruits rolled to the edge of the table and crashed to the floor into what sounded like a million pieces. Undaunted, Cody didn't stop to pick up his mess. Instead, he used the table as an anchor and eased his way around it.

His foot slipped on a wet spot on the tile floor and he fell hard to one knee, wincing at the pain that shot through his leg.

"Oh, my goodness, Cody. Are you all right?" Isadore was behind him. "All this water on the floor. Let me help you."

"Don't touch me." With his hands in front of him, Cody crawled along the floor, trying to distinguish the direction Lyssa had taken. The puddles turned to the left. Toward the kitchen stairway that led to the second floor.

"I didn't hear you come into the house," Isadore

was saying, but Cody wasn't listening. His hand slipped on the wet surface beneath his palms and he went down again, this time smacking his shoulder and his cheek on the floor. Instead of defeating him, the pain only fueled an already burning anger.

"You're going to hurt yourself." Isadore's voice was just short of a cry, but Cody was infinitely glad she didn't attempt to approach him.

The stairs were wet when he reached them. He stood and gripped his hand on the rail and used it to propel himself up two steps at a time. When he reached the landing, he ran his right hand along the smooth walls and counted doors until he reached Lyssa's bedroom.

He leaned on the middle of the door, intending to steady himself just enough not to attack. Instead, the door gave way and he stumbled in, crashing to the floor.

Chapter Three

"The door was closed."

Lyssa tried not to act as alarmed as she was by Cody's sudden intrusion.

She'd needed to get away from him. To clear her head. Heck, to even find it. Never in her life had she acted in such an unprofessional way with a student. It shamed her to think she'd stooped that low. But Cody was just so . . . infuriating. How could he think she'd be so cruel as to intentionally stage a drowning? It was beyond comprehension.

But while her little stomp through the house, soaking wet and fuming, had been enough to cool her unleashed fury, it was clear that hadn't been the case for Cody.

He quickly got to his feet and stared at her. Well, not at her. It was as if he were looking through the haze of a ghost.

"You may have closed the door, but apparently it hadn't shut all the way or I wouldn't have ended up in a heap on your floor."

He had to have flown through the house to have made it to her room this quickly.

"You need to leave, Cody."

"I will. But not until I've finished what I have to say."

"Do it and then please leave."

A vein jumped to life in his neck and his jaw clenched. "This is my home. My sanctuary. I don't care what my father asked of you."

"Your sanctuary, huh? Just how deep does that sanctuary go? How long are you going to stay buried here before you realize you aren't even living?"

The initial intrusion forgotten, Lyssa found her blood pounding stronger than it had been by the pool.

"You have no idea what you're talking about, Lyssa. How could you know if you've never been blind?"

"For your information, Mr. Know-it-all, I was blind for twenty years of my life. I've sat in that dark seat just the same as you, so don't give me that line of crap that I don't know how you feel. I was there!"

Lyssa's voice had risen to a fevered pitch, leaving her ears ringing and her heart pounding. With each word she uttered, she rose up, as if trying to reach the unreachable brass ring.

Cody stopped short.

"You . . . you're blind?"

It took a second for her to draw in a deep breath as she reeled in her anger.

"I was blind at one time. I'm not anymore. And when I was blind I managed to go to school, go shopping, visit my friends, and work a job. This job. I've only been able to see for about four years. And there's nothing I do now that I didn't do when I was blind."

"You just never learned how to swim."

She shook her head and would have laughed at the sarcasm in his voice if she'd been in a better frame of mind.

"I never got around to that."

"Did you ever ride horses?"

"No. I've never been on a horse, either."

He sighed, his shoulders sagging. "Why not?"

"I . . . don't really know. We didn't have horses like you have here. My sister was never interested and frankly, neither were my parents. They're not really the outdoorsy type. I guess I was just never exposed to them."

He nodded.

"Get out of those wet clothes and we'll go riding, then."

It was just like that. His anger was gone. Vanished—as if it were never there.

"Wait. I just told you I've never been on a horse before."

With his hand stretched out in front of him, Cody turned and made his way to the wall, then the doorway. "There's always a first time."

"If I do this, will you stop being so obstinate about working with Otis?"

"You're putting conditions on this?"

"Yes. Or no deal."

Her heart hammered. A horse? Yeah, she liked them, but had never really been within twenty feet of one. Still, she wasn't about to lose the ground she'd gained.

"Deal."

"Good. Give me about a half hour."

"How long does it take you to get out of wet clothes?"

"I need a half hour," Lyssa insisted.

Cody hesitated, then nodded. "I'll meet you downstairs in a half hour then."

Holding the wall, he backed through the doorway and turned toward his bedroom, closing the door behind him.

Lyssa closed her eyes and breathed a sigh of relief. She didn't need the half hour to dry off and dress. That would only take a matter of minutes. She needed the time to compose herself, rid herself of this unsettling feeling that had engulfed her. She hadn't expected to feel the things she'd felt when Cody had held her. She hadn't expected to be so breathless.

Glancing down at herself, she noticed the wide puddle that had collected on the floor around her bare feet. She refused to feel guilty about being glad, just this once, that Cody was blind and couldn't see that the whole time they'd stood there arguing she'd been standing there in dripping wet underwear.

Forget the fact that Cody didn't even ask her if she'd wanted to go riding. His gruff command had been delivered almost as an order. There was something commanding about him, and yet . . .

Normally, it would have ticked her off to no end. But Cody hadn't asked her to come to the ranch and bring Otis with her, either. She'd invaded his world in a way that made him uncomfortable. So maybe this made them even.

Even, my foot, Lyssa thought. How the heck was she going to get on a horse? She'd never been on a horse. And what she knew about them could probably fit on the white space on her newly acquired driver's license.

There's always a first, Lyssa decided. Her adult life had been filled with firsts, not the least of which was today, when Cody was holding her in his arms as he carried her across the pool. Lord help her, she didn't know what had come over her. But there she was, wrapped in muscled arms that felt like steel, and suddenly her head started spinning and she'd caught herself getting breathless. If she hadn't run away when she had she would have ended up making a huge fool of herself.

If Cody was that strong now, she had to wonder how strong he'd been before the accident. If sitting in that chair and doing very little these last months had made his arms feel that strong, what had he been like before?

It was no good. She wasn't thinking of Cody as a student who needed her help and training. She was thinking of him as a man. And that simply couldn't happen. She'd lost her perspective where he was concerned.

Maybe this ride was a good idea. It would get Cody out on his own turf and then later, they could talk reasonably about how to proceed with training. It was a good plan, an even trade of sorts. Why was she filled with so much anxiety?

She'd managed to slip into a fresh pair of jeans that thankfully weren't too tight in the thighs. She could only imagine how graceful she'd be climbing into the saddle in pants that were too snug. She chose a cool white cotton shirt, pulled a brush through her almost dry hair, and pulled it back into a ponytail before heading downstairs.

Cody was waiting for her in the kitchen, a slightly smug look on his face. She wasn't sure what she'd expected, but smug wasn't it. Anticipation maybe? Hadn't Beau mentioned Cody hadn't been riding since the accident?

"Maybe I'm not the best person in the world to go with you on this ride," she said as she drew closer.

"Chickening out already? I expected more from you, Lyssa."

"It's not that. It's just . . . I don't know anything about horses."

There, she'd admitted it. It was no big deal. Lots of people didn't know a lick about lots of things and it didn't make them anything other than ignorant about that subject.

"Yeah, you mentioned you'd never been riding. That's okay. I have."

He turned and opened the screen door, stepping outside and extending his arm out to her. If she hadn't already had a taste of Cody, she'd think he was being polite and asking to escort her to the stables. Maybe that was an automatic gesture for a southern gentleman like him.

But she did know Cody already. Just like the other day, rather than ask for a little help, he was turning the tables on her and making it seem as though he was leading her instead of the other way around. No matter. Survival was survival, and it was good in any form if it worked. And she'd bet next week's salary he was as nervous about getting on that horse as she was.

Well, maybe not. She didn't think anything could rival her nerves right at that moment.

They reached the stables and Beau was already there, saddling up a big old gray horse with dusty spots on his back. She resisted the urge to take a step back when the horse bobbed his big head.

"I didn't know whether you'd want to ride Sassy or not, so I figured I'd wait until you got out here," Beau said.

Lyssa watched Cody move along the wall, following each gate until he reached the third stall. When Sassy neighed, his smile was immediate and transformed his whole face. She had the feeling that just being in the presence of the animal was enough to soften even the roughest edges of this man.

He opened the stall and walked inside, and her heart leaped to her throat. This is what she was trained to do, help people get along with their normal lives, but clearly Cody didn't need any help at all here—especially from her—to do what was completely bred in him. She suspected then, that much of what was keeping him back was his inability to see a normal life again.

She groaned inwardly, thinking about the conversation she'd had with Catherine. Cody Gentry was a tough cookie, but one that needed special attention, and she was just tenacious enough to give him what he needed.

Somehow Lyssa doubted that. Cody didn't need anything at all from her. Greeting Sassy, watching him search the rail for the blanket to place over the horse's back, made her forget for a split second that Cody had lost his vision. It spoke of a man not searching in the darkness, but of one sure of his step, confident of his place in the world. And she had to admire that.

No, Cody didn't need her out here at all. Everything he did need was locked up inside himself. Maybe this was the key to help him unlock the door.

*   *   *

Getting on the back of Smokin' Diesel E proved more comical than difficult, Lyssa discovered. And when she finally got the hang of holding the reins and leading a horse that clearly didn't need any direction from her, her nerves settled into a somewhat slow and steady pace.

Thankfully, so had the horses and she found herself actually enjoying the ride across the ranch. Cody had said they were taking a trail well traveled, which relieved Lyssa considerably. If they somehow got lost on their way back, she wasn't going to be much help. Her sense of direction was good, but with all the twists and turns the path took, she had to admit she'd lost her bearings.

Cody, on the other hand, just allowed Sweet Sassy's Smile to lead him along the trail as if it was a route they'd taken a thousand times. Which they probably had, Lyssa decided, as she watched how little guidance Cody gave the horse.

"Let me know when we get to the open pasture," he said. "It should be just as we take a sharp turn at the end of the trail."

Sure enough, the trail they'd been riding on ended and opened up into a wide pasture.

Her mouth flew agape. "How on earth did you know where we were?"

Cody just grinned. "I've been riding this trail since I was old enough to sit in the saddle on my own." A soft chuckle escaped his lips and she felt something inside her shift in place, stealing her breath away. "And Sassy always gets a little excited when we get to this point, too. There's a nice stream here with some good grass for grazing. There should be a huge cottonwood with branches that jut out like bony arms in all directions, sitting right about center in this pasture."

It was unmistakable. The enormous cottonwood commanded its place in the middle of the field. There were herds of cattle in different scatterings in the grass. Some clustered by a winding stream, and some huddled together in the only shade available, under a lone tree out in the field.

"If you're ready to take a break, we can stop there a while. Stretch your legs," Cody said.

It was none too soon for Lyssa. They hadn't really been riding all that long, but already her backside was going numb and her thighs were beginning to ache.

They rode to the cottonwood and dismounted. Cody waited until Lyssa had two feet firmly planted on the ground and walked Diesel alongside Sassy.

He loosely secured the reins to the saddle horn and gave a quick little swat to Sassy's behind. Diesel pulled against the reins, intending to follow Sassy.

"Tie the reins up to the saddle horn," Cody said. "This is a good place for them to get some water and graze while we sit a bit."

The temperature difference was marked as Lyssa moved from under the scorching sun into the shade of the cottonwood tree and dropped to the cool grass. Following the sound of her movement on the hard ground, Cody walked behind her and sat on the ground, a good three feet away. Conversationally close, Lyssa realized, but not intimate.

"It's been a long time since I've been out here," he said, his voice a little distant, as if he were lost somewhere else instead of with her. For a moment, she wasn't sure he was even talking to her.

"It's beautiful," she said, looking out into the pasture, taking in the green and sparkle of light from the sun off the stream. Animals were contently grazing as if there was nothing else in the world but them.

"Yeah, it's always been."

"But," she said, forcing the word she knew he was about to say.

"Things have changed."

"Not as much as you think, Cody. Not the core of you. That's still the same."

Despite the sunglasses and the Stetson Cody wore, she could see the tight knit of his brow. "You really believe that?"

"You're just afraid. I don't blame you. Change is never easy for anyone."

"You got your eyesight back."

The way Cody spoke the words, it was as if that made all the difference in the world. And maybe to him it did. But Lyssa knew differently.

"Yeah, I did. But even as wonderful as that is, it wasn't easy. And if you think about it, change, good or bad, is never easy for anyone. Every single day, people get married or divorced and start over. They go off to school, change careers, move across the country, and they're scared as heck. No one is immune.

"Everyone has this place inside them that they lock up all their fears, all the things about them that they're afraid to show to the world."

"I don't."

She couldn't help but smirk. "Sure. Even a what-you-see-is-what-you-get kind of guy like you has fears and you're staring at them now."

He stiffened.

"Yeah, and that's the scariest part," she went on,

not allowing him to deny it. "When you can walk around sure of yourself, you never have to worry about that little box in your soul. You hide it, you nurture it, you may even rage against it sometimes when you're alone. Because it's yours. No one else gets to see it. All those things about yourself that make you uncomfortable, the things about you that you're so sure make you . . . unlovable . . . live there in that little box."

"Really," he said dryly.

She ignored his sarcasm and leaned back with her arms behind her, letting the shade of the tree cool her warmed skin.

"But when you can't see, suddenly it's like everyone around you *can* see what's there deep inside that locked box you've been hiding in your soul. All those things you fear people will judge against you."

"You mean, like not picking up your dirty socks for three weeks."

"Oh, that's disgusting," Lyssa said, laughing. "No, not those little superficial things. It's the things that make you vulnerable. The things that you've convinced yourself no one could possibly love you for. But you know what the greatest thing about love is, the people that love you don't see those things you fear the same way. They don't matter to them the way they do to you."

"What does this have to do with me?"

"Maybe nothing. I don't know, I guess I'm not explaining myself real well. I've never been really good at that." Her shoulders sagged.

"No, it sounds real pretty. I just don't know why you're telling me. I mean, I pick up my dirty socks."

Lyssa laughed again, grabbed a fistful of grass from

the ground, and tossed it at Cody. He flinched slightly when the blades hit his face and then brushed them off with a chuckle.

"I'm sure Isadore comes in behind your back and picks up your dirty socks for you."

"Heck, no, she'd beat me with a bat if I ever expected that. Come on, Lyssa, admit it. You're really a slob, right?"

She laughed again. "No, quite the opposite, I'm afraid. I'm very compulsively organized, but that comes more from conditioning than personality. If even a hairbrush was out of place on my dresser, it used to drive me crazy because I knew it would take me forever to find it. My sister, Kim, used to rearrange my stuff all the time."

He gasped in mock horror. "I'll bet you wouldn't even dare walk into a store through the OUT door."

"Of course not. Do have any idea how hard it would be for blind people if everyone did that?"

"I don't know. A little spontaneous dancing in the doorway with you might be kind of fun."

Lyssa gave up and just let the laughter take hold of her until her belly hurt. "Oh, you really are as impossible as your father warned."

"I pride myself on that."

"I'm sure you do."

Cody was quiet a moment. If she didn't know he was blind, she'd have assumed he was looking out into the pasture and losing himself in the beauty that surrounded them. But Lyssa knew that wasn't the case even before he heaved a slow sigh.

"You're right, you know," he said, his voice quiet against the rush of breeze through the trees. "I don't like what I've become. I can't see what I want to see, and what I do see I don't like."

"Only you can change that."

"I can't unless this next surgery works."

"With or without the surgery you're still the same man."

Lyssa would have missed the almost imperceptible shake of Cody's head if she hadn't been staring at him the way she was.

"Different. I don't . . . know who I am. I've been working this ranch since I was a kid, doing things, I don't know, because that's the way it is. And I didn't go looking for something else. I like what I have here. I just don't know where I fit in here anymore."

"I know this sounds simplistic, but just because you can't look into the mirror and see your reflection doesn't mean it isn't there. You're not invisible."

He swallowed, licked his lips, and turned a fraction of an inch away from her gaze. "I don't know what's there. That's just the point."

He was uncomfortable. Lyssa guessed that was about as much as Cody would reach out to anyone to ask for a hand. She would offer him both of hers and let him decide just how much he could handle. And she would be honest. He deserved to hear the truth.

"Your life is different, I'll give you that. But you're not. The core of who you are hasn't changed. Every value you've had, every goal is the same. You just need to redefine it. Make it work for you now. And you can do that and be happy."

"Were you happy?"

She shook her head and chose her words carefully before she spoke. "You can't really compare the two of us. Our situations are so different. I didn't have the same kind of expectations you have. I simply didn't know anything else. I took what I had and made my life right from the beginning. There was no loss to mourn."

"You think that's what I'm doing?"

"Yes. It's quite common. If you'd opened yourself up to the counseling available—"

Cody groaned and shifted uncomfortably.

Undaunted, Lyssa went on. "You could have worked with people who would have helped you and your family adjust. Lots of people who've become blind as adults do well."

"Doesn't make me feel good to be part of that statistic."

"You're not a statistic, Cody. You're a man. And you need to start looking at yourself that way again. Otherwise, you'll be stuck sitting in a chair for the rest of your life."

He was quiet for a moment, about to say something, hesitating and then retreating. It took a while and she waited.

"I don't want to be a cripple."

"Is that how you see yourself?"

"Don't you?"

"No."

His jaw tightened. "Everyone else around me does."

She closed her eyes, knowing that it was true to some degree. "They won't stop until you do."

When he didn't say anything further, she went on.

"You trust your horse. Why can't you trust Otis? He can give you so much more of your life back."

"It's not the same thing. When I'm riding, I'm free. I'm not someone who needs anyone else. I'm not wearing this big sign that says 'Watch out for the blind man.' " His heavy sigh echoed his obvious frustration. "Having a guide dog will just make me look . . ."

"What?"

"I don't know. Less of a man, I guess." His laugh was harsh and filled with contempt. She wasn't quite sure for what. "I guess I'm egotistical enough to want to be able to stand on my own two feet."

"Ego has nothing to do with it. And Otis can help you achieve what you want. It has to be better than what you've been going through. I just don't understand why you won't at least give it a try."

"I don't need him. It would be a waste of both his time and yours. This next transplant is going to work."

Lyssa clamped her teeth down on her bottom lip, her own frustration getting the better of her.

"I hope it does, Cody. I really do. The advances in eye surgery have been tremendous these last few years. But I know the percentage of corneal transplants that take successfully after a burn like yours is only about five to eight percent, and you've already had one rejection. Aren't you afraid of setting yourself up for even bigger disappointments by not facing even the possibility of what you'll do if this next surgery doesn't work?"

"No," Cody said resolutely.

"Then you're not being very realistic. Or fair to yourself."

"Life isn't fair, in case you haven't noticed."

"No, it's not. But you can at least be fair to yourself even when life throws you a curve."

"What do you look like?" he asked, pulling at the grass clippings that formed a soft blanket on the ground around them.

Thrown by his abrupt change of subject, she said, "Why do you ask?"

He shrugged. "Curiosity, I guess. When I talk to most people, even my doctor, who I met years before losing my vision, I have a picture in my head of what they look like. Even if I can't see them, there is something to call up from my memory. I think I can pretty much figure out what Otis looks like."

Lyssa smirked. "He's much more beautiful than the average dog."

"I'll take your word for it. And I'll bet he's a heck of a kisser, but I'm going to take your word on that too. With you, though, I can't make a picture. It's like a blank slate."

"Well, there you go. I'm a faceless person sent out here to drive you crazy."

That earned her a laugh. A real one that seemed to bubble up from his belly right out into the wind. He had a nice laugh. She wondered if it was something the rest of his family missed hearing from him these last few months.

"I gotta tell you, I'm spending a huge amount of time wondering what you look like."

"You've had some time on your hands, I'll give you that."

Cody groaned. "Too much. I don't like that." His complaint was one of frustration, Lyssa knew. Without knowing Cody all that much, she'd already deduced that he had never been a man to sit idle before the accident. Not if he could help it. Most of what she'd seen on the ranch Cody had had some hand in the making. All this excess time must be driving him more crazy than she ever could.

She shifted to make herself more comfortable in the

grass, tucking her legs up underneath her. Although she had no idea how she could get comfortable in this conversation.

"Does it really matter what I look like?" Deep down, Lyssa knew that it did. She'd seen firsthand the moment her eyes opened up to the world, being able to see reaction rather than just sense it. She had forgiven Chad a long time ago for falling for Kim.

And her sister, how could she fault her for being born with the beautiful gene? Somehow in the massive mix of gene distribution, Kim had been blessed with thick, flowing blond hair, enormous blue eyes, and a face with natural beauty that required absolutely no care. Kim transformed a pair of baggy sweatpants into runway fashion in a way Lyssa could only envy.

There were times when Lyssa would look in the mirror and catch the clear blue, nondescript eyes, straight, sandy blond hair, and simple features, and wonder how the random distribution of genes had passed her by so unfairly. She wasn't ugly by any stretch. She just wasn't beautiful.

She knew it shouldn't matter. Beauty was in the eye of the beholder. But she also knew it did matter to some people. It had mattered to Chad.

Lyssa quietly sighed and decided to stop thinking about Chad and what she lacked in life. She'd long ago learned to stuff those feelings into her own secret box and hide them away. It was much more crippling to let them win.

She had been blessed with something much more important in life. She got her vision back. What else could compare to that?

"It's no big deal, really," Cody was saying. "Like I said, I was just wondering. I mean, I can't imagine how you did it. Didn't you ever wonder what people looked like? What colors were? That must have been incredible, you know, the first time you opened your eyes and saw the world. I can't imagine it."

Lyssa shrugged. "It was pretty amazing." The heady feeling she'd initially felt that first day enveloped her again with the memory. "I didn't remember ever seeing before the accident."

"So you weren't born blind?"

"No, like you, I had an accident. Unfortunately, my father was killed. My real father, that is. Mom remarried when I was a little over three years old and all I remember growing up was my stepdad."

Nathan Jones had never adopted her, although Lyssa had never seen the need. She was his daughter in every way that counted. But there were times she wondered why he hadn't adopted her. When she was twelve years old, she had asked her mother about it. She couldn't see her mother's face, but sensed the sudden, subtle, sadness in the tone of her voice. Her mother had truly loved Lyssa's real dad. She explained that allowing her stepdad to adopt Lyssa would be like taking away the precious gift Brian McElhannon had given her, erasing his very existence.

When Lyssa could finally see, she'd sifted through boxes of baby pictures and photo albums and looked at her biological father's face for the first time. She looked exactly like him, and she finally understood.

"What was the first thing you saw?"

Lyssa smiled. "My mother. My vision didn't come back all at once. There were several surgeries over a period of time. I remember it starting out as a haze and then things slowly came into view. I knew my mother's voice so well, but I was stunned by her face and how beautiful she was. I remember staring at her for the longest time and then my sister, then my dad. Although by the time I got to my dad I had so many tears in my eyes I couldn't see much of anything."

She chuckled and swallowed a small lump that lodged in her throat.

"The first night I absolutely refused to go to sleep because I thought it was all a dream and I'd wake up blind again."

"Was it anything like you thought it would be?"

"Yes and no." Some things were *very* different.

"That's a good answer."

She laughed again and stood up, brushing the dry grass from her jeans.

"Faces intrigued me. Even sculpting never gave me a clear image in my mind."

"What's that?"

"What?"

"Sculpting. Are you talking about with clay?"

She shook her head. "With your hands. Touching something and then forming the image in your mind. Kind of like a hands-on sonogram. Most people did have blank faces to me, but the people I was close to usually let me sculpt them. That's what I called it anyway. I could feel what they looked like."

"With your hands."

"Yes, just like a real sculptor uses clay."

"How you do that?"

Cody seemed to be hanging on her every word and, for the first time since she'd arrived at the ranch, seemed very interested in what she had to say.

"I would touch their face, glide my fingers over their features, and commit them to memory. Kind of like an instant Polaroid."

"Will you show me?"

"What do you mean 'show you?' I can't really show you." She let out a quick laugh, mostly out of nervousness. Was he serious?

"Sure you can. You aren't afraid, are you?"

"No, of course not." Absolutely! Sculpting was not something she'd ever done with a stranger. Sure, Cody wasn't really a stranger anymore, but he certainly wasn't somebody she felt close enough to to touch in that way.

"Then what's the problem?" he asked.

"I can't accurately show you without . . ."

"Touching me? That is kind of the point, isn't it?"

His mouth lifted to one side in a devilish grin. This was a side of Cody she hadn't yet seen. Teasing, playful, and knowing full well he was getting to her.

Darn him.

"I've never shown someone how to do it before. Besides, it's no big deal."

"If it's no big deal, then I don't see the problem. Come on, I'm not going to bite. Just close your eyes and do it to me. I want to know how it's done."

Her pulse quickened, but she couldn't fathom why. Why did he do this to her?

She sat back down on the grass under the sturdy arms of the shady tree. She was knee-to-knee with Cody, and had to lean forward with her arms stretched to reach him. He seemed to sense the problem and moved in closer, resting his hands on her knees. Leaning forward, she placed her hands on his cheek.

"Wait," Cody said, straightening just a little.

"What's wrong?" She had barely touched him.

"I want to do it to you too."

"After I show you—"

"No, at the same time," he said resolutely.

"Okay."

She was surprised by how quickly her answer escaped her lips. The thought of Cody touching her, even something so innocent as touching her face, sent a shiver zipping through her. Not out of fear, but anticipation.

She'd felt his control, his strength, in the pool and it had taken her time to get over the effect it had on her.

It wasn't as if this was the first time she'd been touched this way by a man. She had sculpted with Chad before, and why wouldn't she? They'd been dating a long time by then and she was curious about everything about him.

Somehow, with Cody, Lyssa knew it would be very different.

Chapter Four

Lyssa closed her eyes and silently sucked in a deep breath when she took Cody's hands in her much smaller ones and guided them to her warm cheeks. It had been more than four years since she'd sculpted with anyone. The last time had been with Chad.

In the darkness it had been easy. She didn't see Chad's reaction, she felt everything. In an ironic twist, her eyes got in the way now. Her sense of touch wasn't as strong as it had once been. But Cody's was. And she still remembered all too well the feelings of intimacy that collided with her senses in reaction to just a simple touch.

"Just do what I do," she said, her voice just above a whisper.

"That should be easy enough."

Easier said than done, Lyssa thought. At least for him. Cody's fingers weren't trembling like she knew hers were. Just being this close to Cody had made Lyssa's heart hammer inside her chest more than getting on that horse ever could.

"I always started at the top of the head."

She pulled off his hat and placed it on the soft, green grass by his side. He took off his glasses, placed them inside the hat, and closed his eyelids.

"Ever so lightly touch the skin until . . ."

And then she did it. She'd actually sighed like a lovesick teenager gazing up at the star high school basketball player. When Cody didn't react as if he'd noticed, relief washed over her flaming cheeks.

His hands were big, his palms wide, but his touch was remarkably delicate. It made Lyssa wonder what it would be like to be held in those hands. Not like today when he'd held her out of fear that she was drowning. He'd been frightened then, moving frantically and quickly because he'd thought she was hurt.

Now Cody was touching her in a way that spoke of gentleness and control. Quite different, but it surprised Lyssa that her reaction to his touch was the same.

He gently pulled at the elastic band keeping her ponytail in place. She had to counter his move by leaning forward so she wouldn't lose balance. And then his fingers were in her hair, touching her lightly, pulling at little strands, rolling them between his fingers and the pad of his thumb all the way to their ends.

"Your hair is shorter than I imagined, silkier. And it seems to be all one length."

Lyssa cleared her throat, afraid to try her voice. "Yes, that's right. My forehead isn't that high and—"

"Ssh . . ." he said quietly, his voice blending in with the breeze while he lightly traced his fingers over her eyelids. "I want to figure it out for myself. Do you always wear your hair up?"

"Not always."

Her hands had stopped moving, settled on the square of his jaw. She was too distracted by what Cody was doing and how his touch made her feel.

"Wait, this isn't working."

Thank you, God. Lyssa didn't know how much more of this sweet torture she could take.

"Drop your hands. I think I have the hang of this. Just let me touch you."

"Okay."

She fiddled with her hands in her lap as Cody continued to move.

"You have narrow eyes. What color are they?"

"Blue."

"Blue like what?"

She shrugged. What could she really say? Growing up, women are taught to love themselves the way the are, but it was human nature to pick yourself apart when it was only you looking in the mirror. To actually have to describe herself and be honest was just too weird. Still, for the sake of fair play, she gave it a try.

"They're not a dark blue. My sister Kim has dark blue eyes that remind me of sapphires."

His hands stilled, cupping her cheeks. "I'm not asking about your sister. I want to know you."

She really didn't want to pull out the list of flaws she'd cataloged over the past few years.

"Lighter, not really like the sky, but—"

"Slate, smoky?"

"I guess. Yes. But they're kind of wide-set."

A smile stretched his lips. He brushed the pad of his thumb over her eyelashes, forcing her to close her eyes.

"Your cheekbones are very prominent. And you like to laugh. I can feel the laugh lines."

With his hands still cupping her cheeks, his fingers gently caressed her earlobes. A crease puckered between his eyebrows. "No earrings?"

"I never got them pierced."

"I find that strange."

"Why?"

"I don't know. Girls like jewelry and all those dainty things."

Lyssa didn't want to mention the dainty things he missed seeing earlier. Her one and only true vice was fine underwear. The best. It had always been that way. She loved to feel it beneath her clothes. If she had money in her pocket to buy either a dress or some lingerie, she chose the latter, which was maybe why most of her wardrobe consisted of blue jeans and cotton shirts. It wasn't very alluring to the opposite sex, she knew, but it made her feel good.

Wearing casual clothes made it easier to work with the dogs. She didn't have to worry about ruining her clothes, even though her mother always complained it made her look too boyish.

That may be true, but it was the sleek silk underneath her denim blues that made Lyssa feel feminine. However, that particular detail wasn't likely to come up in conversation between her and Cody any time soon.

"I don't wear any jewelry when I'm working with dogs. Which is pretty much all the time."

"You're not working with any dogs right now," he challenged her with a grin.

"It's become a habit. I don't even think about it most of the time, unless someone brings it up."

She closed her eyes and tried to steady her breathing as the pad of his thumbs made a slow pass over her lips. Then another.

"And I'm guessing no lipstick either."

"That's right."

His lips tilted into a grin. "Generous mouth."

She laughed at that. "Some would say a little too generous. In size and opinion."

Lyssa sat there with Cody on the grass beneath the shady tree. He forced her eyes closed with his fingers. All of her senses seemed to explode to life. In the distance she heard the sound of grazing cattle, the rustle of leaves blowing over bony roots protruding from the ground. If she was quiet enough she could swear she could hear the hammer of own heart beating with Cody's.

He said her name so softly Lyssa wasn't sure she had actually heard it at all. But then his fingers cupped her cheeks again and she opened her eyes.

Cody sat there, his lips just inches from hers. His eyes were closed, his mouth slightly parted, his lips moist. He was going to kiss her. That realization sparked a flame so deep and hot inside her it stole her breath away. She had been so caught up in how she felt that she hadn't been paying attention at all to Cody's reaction. And the fact that touching her this way had affected him too only made her senses burn brighter.

She shouldn't be so shocked, but she was. It wasn't as if she hadn't imagined what it would be like to kiss Cody. In truth, she had. The past three nights had seemed very long, leaving her anxious and wondering about the kind of man Cody really was. Not just now,

but before the accident, before his life had been de-
railed so drastically.

She had seen many people bounce back from similar tragedies, although it was never easy. It took a
certain amount of inner strength that made a person
put one foot in front of the other. Those whose situations made it seem near certain they wouldn't suc-
ceed were usually the ones who surprised her the most.
That inner strength of character drove them beyond
what was believed possible.

Cody had that inner strength. Lyssa knew it. There
was something so strong about him, so determined,
and yet he somehow had succumbed to the idea that
his life was over.

And now here he was clearly wanting something
that she herself had dreamed of these past three nights.
She wanted to kiss him, wanted to feel what it was
like to press her lips against his and discover the mystery, feel the engine that burned inside him roar to life.

For her this time.

He said her name again, this time louder, and it was
clear to Lyssa that he was waiting, waiting for her to
lean in and except his invitation.

She ran her tongue over her lips, feeling the cool
breeze brush over them as the wind blew.

His hands lingered on her cheeks, touching her
softly in silence. He held her face in his hands with
such care it made her dizzy. Then he abruptly dropped
them to his lap.

"You're a very beautiful woman, Alyssandra." His
voice was so low and deep that she could barely hear
it over the neighs of the horses, the distant moos of
cattle, and the rustling of leaves in the trees.

Tears immediately sprang to Lyssa's eyes. Not because she didn't believe Cody. In his mind, maybe he *had* taken the simple, plain woman she was in reality and turned her into something beautiful in his mind. And for that moment, she did feel as beautiful as he seemed to believe.

At first, he didn't move away, and didn't say another word. He just sat there, oh, so close, opposite her on the grass. All Lyssa could think of was the way he'd held her face in his hands as if she were a fragile piece of glass.

And then he did move away, leaning back with his arms behind him, as if he was actually gazing out at the pasture beyond them.

Already she missed the feel of his hands and was disappointed the brief link they'd shared was now broken. Regret washed over her and she only hoped Cody couldn't hear it in her voice.

"Thank you," he murmured.

"For what?"

"For letting me see you. For making me feel alive for the first time in eight months."

She smiled, feeling a heat swell in her chest and creep up her neck. "You're welcome."

"Tell me what you see. The pasture, I mean."

She looked out at the field. "It's breathtaking. But you know that already."

"Yes, I do know. But I want to hear it from you. I want to see it through your eyes. It's different to sit here like I have my whole life and look at these pastures.

"People tend to take things for granted when they know all they have to do is reach out and grab something and it's theirs. It loses meaning. It's different looking at something for the first time. Don't you think?"

"I suppose you're right."

Lyssa gazed out at the rippling fields of sunlit gold and green. The hills rolled all the way across the pasture until they reached a wooded area.

"The branches of this tree stretch out and form a sort of shaded cave. A few cattle are huddled underneath a similar tree on the rise of one of the hills, but most of the herd is huddled together out in the field."

"But where are we?"

"There is a dirt road that cuts through the far right-hand side of the pasture and heads into the wooded area that goes to the hills. Patches of beautiful wildflowers are all blooming on one side of it."

"And on the other side of the road is a flat grassy spot?"

She smiled. "Yes."

"Take me there."

She glanced at him then, saw the bittersweet smile playing at the corners of his lips. It almost seemed as if he was at war with it.

She didn't relish the idea of getting back on that horse, although she had to admit that old Diesel was as gentle as a kitten, despite his size. But this time she didn't have a stool to stand on to help her hoist herself into the saddle. Which meant only one thing. Cody had to help her. And without his vision she wondered how what seemed comical earlier could be frustrating now.

There was only one way to find out.

Cody needed a distraction. He hadn't been kidding when he said this was the first time in eight months he truly felt alive. It had taken every bit of willpower he had to hold himself back and not kiss Lyssa. Sure, there was a lot of steam and sass in Lyssa, but something told him this wasn't a woman who knew the rules of the game. There was a definite innocence floating just beneath the surface of her that Cody found hard to ignore. That he found enticing.

He extended his hand, and she easily slipped hers into it. It didn't feel as if she was leading him when she didn't readily release his grip. And he liked that about her. He didn't feel this crippling sense of need. At least, not the kind of need that ate at his soul.

With their hands entwined, he couldn't help but think of the feel of his hands on Lyssa's face, feeling her soft, warm breath against his palm. How it nearly did him in.

As if she was oblivious to the war raging inside him, Lyssa just walked, and he followed until the sounds of hooves dropping to the dirt and jaws chomping grew louder.

A light breeze cooled his cheeks and brought Lyssa's scent with it. She was standing right beside him. Above the more familiar smell of animals and baking grass was a faintly sweet smell that he'd come to associate with Lyssa.

Before she could move out of his way, his hands were around her waist. And for a second, he'd forgotten why they were standing there in the field. He wanted to kiss her, feel his mouth cover hers and feel her explode beneath his touch.

"I'll lift you up," he said, not giving her the chance to protest.

"Okay. But then you'll need to find your horse."

"That's not a problem."

It hadn't taken a whole lot of effort to lift her. Having been in the saddle once already she knew the drill. He took the extra moment to stroke Diesel E's neck while waiting for her prompt.

"Sassy's just a few yards to your left. I'll guide you there."

He wanted to tell her that all he had to do was whistle and Sassy would be by his side. But that hadn't been a cue between the two of them in many months. Cody couldn't be sure that Sassy would remember the way it used to be with them.

Regret ran strong through his veins, soaking him hard from head to foot. He'd stayed away too long. Animals were forgiving. But he'd let go of something precious that he loved, not trusting it would be there for him when he needed it the most. He hadn't been fair to either one of them.

So Diesel E led the way and before he knew it, Sassy was standing beside him, waiting patiently for him to mount. His sunglasses hid the unbidden tears that sprung to his eyes. Thank God some things were as sure as the sunrise. Too bad his faith hadn't been.

Within the next minute they were riding and he remembered how he loved sitting in the saddle.

"Where are we now?"

"Just at the edge of the road, on the flat grassy area we came in on."

"Good."

His lips stretched into a wide grin before he could help himself. The regret he'd felt just moments ago was replaced by something more potent. Reaching up, he pulled down his hat extra tight on his head.

"How much distance do you figure we have until we hit the trees?"

"Oh, a good quarter of a mile at least, I'd guess. Maybe more."

"Enough. Perfect," he said, mostly under his breath, anticipation racing through him. "Stay here, Lyssa. I'll be right back."

All it took was one quick kick of the stirrups against his horse's ribs, and like lightning striking quick and hot, Sassy took off. Cody and Sassy had run this stretch at least a hundred times. Many times with Cody's eyes closed. He didn't need to see where he was going now. Didn't need to gauge the distance from the house to the pool to the corral and then back again by counting steps. Here he could just fly, and he knew Sassy would take him exactly where he wanted to go.

For the first time in eight months, with nothing to cage him, Cody flew.

Chapter Five

Cody didn't need to hide behind his sunglasses here. He didn't have to pretend. He could simply close his eyes as he had hundreds of times and see the blur of trees and wildflowers race by him while he took in their fragrant scent. The heat tore into his cotton shirt as the wind ruffling his sleeves cooled it down.

Cody wasn't blind here on this little patch of earth. He was alive. And for the first time in a long time, he actually felt whole again. He didn't need a hand to hold, didn't need a worried eye, steady and sure, on his back to make sure he didn't wander into dangerous territory. It was just him and Sweet Sassy's Smile chasing the wind.

Sassy slowed down as they reached the edge of the clearing. Cody knew immediately that they had come to the end of their run. Disappointment consumed him, but he immediately squashed it down. As if driving home the fact that he couldn't look back to see the distance he had just come, the sun beat down unmercifully hard on him, burning the newly cooled skin beneath his shirt.

It would do no good to sink back into the depths of depression. Truth was, it felt too darn good to ride again. All the stubbornness in the world didn't make up for how good he had felt just a few seconds ago. Cody wasn't willing to give that up. Not just yet. He might have to accept his lot in life, but he could take the gift that God had given him and enjoy it for all it was worth.

Finally he understood exactly what Lyssa had been trying to tell him for the past few days. It was still a bitter pill to swallow, and Cody wasn't quite sure his throat was big enough to handle it, but he was sure going to try. If he didn't, there'd never be moments like he'd just experienced. Both with Lyssa and riding Sweet Sassy's Smile. The thought of missing those moments was somehow too hard to accept.

A cluster of honeybees and dragonflies were buzzing among the wildflowers, talking among each other in their way, singing against the backdrop of grazing cattle. He could hear this clearly as if they were right against his ear. In between the clip-clopping of horse hooves against the dry earth he heard another set of hooves charging across the field, coming closer with every second.

What the heck was she thinking?

Cody launched himself from Sassy's saddle and held tight to the reins. This unpredictable woman was out of her ever-loving mind! First time on a horse and she charges after him as if she'd been riding her whole life.

He squashed the feeling of terror that seized him hard. Lyssa had no idea what she was doing, and he could offer her no help at all if she somehow fell from her horse. All it would take was for Diesel to get spooked by a snake and he'd throw her. If she hurt herself, somehow became unconscious, how the heck would he ever find her in all this . . . space?

Cody pushed the unbidden image of Lyssa lying in the tall grass, hurt, unable to move. He didn't want to go there. It wouldn't help her and as of yet, nothing had happened.

The sound of horse hooves slowing to a trot had him praying Lyssa was still secure in the saddle. As relief tumbled over him, Cody tried not to think about how much it must have hurt Lyssa to sit there in that saddle, her behind bouncing up and down, her feet barely in the stirrups.

"Oh, my God, Cody! Are you all right?" she asked, her words coming out in short bursts. She was breathless, scarcely able to speak at all. As if she'd just run the length of the field instead of riding it.

Another vision, quick as a kick to his gut, hit Cody hard, wiping away the fear he'd felt just moments ago. He could almost see the rise and fall of Lyssa's chest as she drew in each achingly strong breath.

He pulled off his hat and dragged his hand over his face as another thought bowled him over. Lyssa was still here. Still putting up with him after all these days of him being a horse's behind. The woman had to have a mother load of gumption. He couldn't help but admire her because of it.

He suspected there was a bit of untamed wildness about Lyssa. Something she hadn't yet begun to explore. And nothing he could say was going to change that, not now. Not that he wanted to.

"Good Lord, Lyssa, I was just about to ask you that very same question. What were you thinking, riding across the field that way?"

"Me?"

"The way you came flying across the field I figured the cavalry must have been chasing my boot heels."

"You were the one that took off like a bullet," she challenged.

"I'm used to that sort of thing. But you aren't. Why didn't you stay back there like I told you to?"

"You were heading straight for the trees. I thought you were going to kill yourself. I thought you'd . . ." Her words trailed off as she drew in more breath.

He couldn't believe how much he was enjoying this. She was actually afraid for him. It was kind of sweet, or would be if it didn't annoy him just a little bit too.

"This is my turf, Lyssa. If there is one thing you don't have to be afraid of here, it's me being in the saddle. I was born here." He gestured to the length of pasture he just ridden but couldn't see. "This is as much a part of me as my fingerprints. That's never going to change, no matter what the world throws me."

"You were riding a horse, Cody." She spoke the words as if that made all the difference in the world.

He asked the obvious. "Your point?"

She grunted with frustration. In his mind, he conjured up an image of her fists balled by her side and the delicate chin he'd had the delightful opportunity to stroke jutting out just enough to show him she was ticked off.

A sweet gust of breeze blew past him, bringing with it the scent of vanilla, her scent. When he'd been sitting close to her under the cottonwood the perfume had filled his head and made it spin. Just as it had that first day by the pond. Now it was mixed with the smell of pasture and animal sweat. But it was there, and it had the same effect it did when he'd been sitting so close to her.

Diesel moved closer, and so did the sound of Lyssa's voice. "You mean to tell me you trust Sassy not to go charging into those woods and taking your head off with the first low branch you pass?"

"That's right."

She was still on the horse, he realized. He could tell by the direction of her voice, and he sensed by the slight unsteadiness of her tone that she didn't want to be there. The ride across the pasture had shaken her to the core.

Cody took one step and reached out a hand. He dropped Sassy's reins so he could move in the direction he thought Diesel E was standing without spooking either animal. Moving his fingers up alongside the horse's sweaty shoulder, he met with Lyssa's thigh. His hand connected with her elbow and he gripped it tight. Without a word she slipped down into his arms. Despite the heat, he wrapped both arms around her and crushed her against his body.

He felt it then. The strong hammer of her heart colliding against the walls of her chest was unmistakable. There was a raging storm inside Lyssa trying to burst free from its barriers. It had to have scared her to death to fly across the field the way she had. But she had done it.

"Can you catch your breath?" he asked.

"I was afraid for you," she said, her voice hitching.

"Then I guess we're even."

His words fell flat and gave him none of the satisfaction he thought they would. He didn't want to get even with Lyssa, he realized. He wanted something else. Something strong and raw, a desire he hadn't had for a very long time. He had the incredible urge to reach out and slip his fingers through her hair just as he had earlier, to touch her silky soft skin and feel her body respond to his fingers.

God help him—the way her heart was racing now, he wanted it to race like that for him. He wanted her breathless and shaking and utterly clinging to him, not out of fear or pity, but from his kiss. He wanted her like this, wrapped in his arms so he could chase the wildness he knew was locked up inside of her. He might not be able to see her with his eyes, but he did get a clear glimpse of what Alyssandra McElhannon was all about.

Cody swallowed hard. He couldn't see her face and he wondered what she was thinking. It still amazed him how many emotions were lost to him, how much the spoken word could be colored by the twitch of lips, the lingering blink of the eyes, the almost imperceptible dip of a gaze.

"You can trust your horse," she said quietly. "Why can't you trust Otis?"

"Nothing against the dog."

"You just don't like his occupation and what it means to you."

"Something like that."

Her sigh was slow and weighted with emotion. "Do you always pass judgment on something before you have even given it a chance? Or is that sort of prejudice reserved only for animals?"

"I can't help the way I feel, Lyssa."

"But your life could be so much richer than it is now."

"How do you feel, Lyssa?"

"What do you mean?"

"You know what I mean. How did it feel charging across that field?"

She was silent for a second or two. Then she chuckled, low and sweet, and Cody knew she was smiling. Now that he'd had the opportunity to feel her smile, he knew what it was like. He held himself back from reaching up and cupping her cheeks so he could feel it again.

"I don't think I've ever been more terrified in all my life."

"What else?"

She laughed. It was small at first, then it grew until he could feel her shoulders shaking from it, feel the rumble inside her chest.

"It was kind of exciting. I'll give you that much."

The wide smile that stretched across Cody's face also brought an aching to his heart.

"A rush," he whispered.

"Yeah."

His voice was low when he spoke again. "If you're not feeling that incredible rush every day, then you're not really living, Lyssa. That's all I'm saying. I want that rush. I want to feel alive again."

"Then stop being afraid to live. Get on your horse and go back to doing what you love."

"It's not that easy. With cuttin', I need my eyes and I don't have them anymore. I can't see the cattle moving in front of me. I can't tell my horse which cow to cut from the herd or what direction to move in because I don't know which way to go. If she stops short because a cow is changing direction I'm liable to fly over her head."

Lyssa's shoulders sagged slightly. "You're looking

at things from inside the box, Cody. Jump out of the box and you are going to get your life back."

"Is that what you did, Lyssa?"

"This isn't about me."

"Yes, it is. You've been there."

She hesitated a moment. "Yes."

"Then you're fooling yourself big-time, Lyssa. Because if this is the first time you've felt that rush since you were able to see, then you're not living at all."

They rode back to the ranch in virtual silence. Every clip-clop of the horse's hooves grated on Lyssa's already frazzled nerves. Annoyance rose up to her throat, bitter and strong, choking her.

Of course she was living, she thought. What else did Cody think she'd been doing her whole life? Her life was full. She did more now than she ever had. Sure, she didn't travel much. She didn't frequent the local bars and cowboy hangouts like Kim seemed to do since she moved away to college.

So she'd never ridden a horse before today. So what? Lots of people had never been on horses. She'd never skydived either, but that didn't mean one day she wouldn't. Although she had to admit taking a running leap out of a plane wasn't high on her to-do list, and probably wouldn't be for a very long time. But just because she hadn't, it didn't mean she wasn't living.

There was a first time for everything. This was Lyssa's first day riding. She wasn't sure there'd be a second time, but at least she had tried.

Maybe it was unfair to be annoyed with Cody. After all, their lives were so totally different. They shared a common bond of blindness, but that's pretty much where their similarities ended.

What annoyed Lyssa most was that beneath it all, there was a grain of truth to what Cody had said. As petrified as she had been flying through that field, it had been thrilling. And that wasn't a feeling she felt very often at all.

Okay, never. She could at least admit it to herself if she didn't have the guts to admit it to Cody. She'd never felt that rush he spoke of.

Except with him, she realized with startling realization. Lately, it seemed that's all she felt when she was with Cody.

Beau was in the arena when they returned. As they passed by the open door, she could hear the sounds of riled cattle moving inside and heavy hoof beats pounding on dirt.

Cody's head turned and paused for a fraction of a second with the sound, a bittersweet smile tugging at his cheeks.

"What is he doing?"

"Working one of the cutting horses," said Cody. "Do you want to go in and watch for a while?"

He shook his head, stiffening his posture as if he'd been unaware he'd done anything at all for her to notice.

"I've never seen a cutting horse in action. I'm curious."

He nodded once, coolly. "Then be my guest. I can find my way back to the house."

"Oh, no. You are not going to hide in that room. We had a deal."

His shoulders sagged just a little, then straightened

as he nodded. "Yes, we did. And I intend to keep my word. But I didn't say anything about cuttin'."

Okay, she'd give him that. But as soon as she showed Cody how to leash Otis and they began their first journey together in the yard, Lyssa was determined to make sure the arena was high on the list of places they explored.

Otis and Cody were a good match, Lyssa realized immediately. She'd worried initially because everything about this situation proved different than the usual circumstances she worked under. Normally, when a student applied for a guide dog and was accepted into the program, they attended a twenty-five day training session at the school with their chosen guide dog. At that point, the dog was with the student 24/7 while a trainer watched to make sure both dog and new handler worked well together.

Mike Gentry's insistence that Cody needed one-on-one attention had skewed things a little. The fact that he'd failed to reveal Cody's lack of interest in working with a guide dog was disturbing, but something had changed. At least for the moment, to Lyssa's great relief.

It wasn't unheard of to train a handler in their own environment, but for Lyssa it was a first.

A first for many things, it seemed.

For now, she was content to watch Cody and Otis begin their bonding as handler and guide dog. Cody was a natural. And Otis, a consummate professional. It was going to work out.

Even if it killed her.

* * *

"It wouldn't kill you to walk beside me," Cody said, his voice dripping with the first bit of annoyance she'd heard in days.

The last three days had proved less irritating than the first few she'd experienced on the ranch. She and Cody would have a morning ride and then spend the afternoon working with Otis. It was a nice compromise, and Lyssa found she was not only getting used to riding, she even found herself looking forward to it.

There had been a major transformation in Cody since the first day they'd gone riding. Gone was the animosity that had plagued him the first few days. There were times now, when they were riding or sitting out on the porch at night talking, that Lyssa forgot her reason for being here.

Cody hadn't, which was good. He seemed to throw himself into training with Otis, listening to her instructions ranging from dog care and basic commands, to how to correct the dog when he made a wrong choice.

Most of the time, Cody was agreeable, focused and cooperative. Unless she was walking a pace or two behind him on his right side.

"If I'm too close, it'll be confusing for Otis. I have to sever the tie with him. He needs to know that he's working with you now and can't take direction from me."

"Did you train him?"

"Yes. We were a team for about a year. He was with another handler, but unfortunately the man passed away and Otis was returned to the school. Some dogs are owned by the school and will go back to move on to new handlers if they're not old enough to retire."

"So if I get my eyesight back after this surgery, Otis will go back to the school."

A knot fisted itself in Lyssa's stomach. "Actually, no. The arrangement your father made with the school was for ownership. It's not uncommon. It's simply a personal choice some people make. Not all handlers own their guide dogs."

Lyssa couldn't quite bring herself to talk about the possibility of what Cody would choose to do with Otis if he did get his eyesight back. It was never easy giving up a friend you've come to love. She knew that firsthand. She did it with her guide dogs all the time.

Instead, she said, "Otis is one of my best dogs."

"But they're all special."

She laughed at the slight drip of sarcasm in his tone.

"Yes, they are. But Otis . . . well, you're not supposed to have favorites, but he has a special place in my heart."

They walked along the brick path that wound around the side of the house leading to the arena. Cody had avoided this route every day since they'd started training. She didn't know why he'd chosen to proceed today.

"Remember the commands I told you about," she instructed. "In your head, think about where you want to go."

"I thought Otis was supposed to do all the thinking. Know whether or not to proceed."

"He's trained to assess the situation you're in, make sure he leaves enough clearance for you to get by, and find the easiest route for you to travel. He'll make sure you don't walk into a hole or cross the street in front of a car. But you're a team. You can't just rely on him to do the work. You need to use your ears and common sense to let him know where *you* want to go."

Otis halted on his own and Cody tried to tug him forward, but he wouldn't budge.

"Why did he stop?"

"There's a curb. It's deep enough that you'll stumble over it. He's warning you of it and waiting for your command before proceeding. Inch forward until you feel the edge and give him the command."

"So you're telling me that if we were in downtown Fort Worth and I tried to cross a road in oncoming traffic, he wouldn't let me?"

"That's right. He's trained to disobey a command from his handler if proceeding presents a danger to him. He can't read crossing signs or see lights change color because dogs don't see that way. But he can see oncoming traffic. Remember, you're a team. You need to work together to assess all situations."

"Any elevator shafts nearby?"

"Very funny," Lyssa said wryly.

"What about a black cat?"

"Are you superstitious?"

He chuckled. "Seriously. Out here at the ranch there could be any number of animals running around. How do I know he's not going to lead me on a wild goose chase of his own liking?"

"He's trained to ignore all distractions, even animals, and become completely in tune with you. The longer he's here, the more used to it he'll be."

"And he can go anywhere?"

"Absolutely. Legally Otis is allowed in any public place that you'd be allowed. However, there may be times when you might choose to keep him home. However trained, he is a dog and there may be situations you feel may pose a danger to him or may be too distracting to him. But if you do take him with you and someone gives you trouble, you should report it."

For the first time in days, Cody had led her close enough to the arena to give him a gentle nudge in the direction that seemed to cause him the greatest fear. The door was open and she could hear people working inside. She took it as a sign that he was ready.

"Show me the arena," Lyssa said, bracing herself for a challenge, and trying to think of a valid argument to counter it.

He seemed to be considering it, his face turned in the direction the sound was coming from.

"I don't want to get in Beau's way," Cody answered.

Lyssa knew Beau would feel Cody's presence to be anything but an intrusion. From the few private conversations they'd shared about Cody, she knew it would be more of a relief than anything.

For all the bickering the two brothers did, Lyssa knew that deep concern and love filtered through. Even on the odd occasions she'd been present when Beau asked Cody advice about one of his horses, Cody's answer was always the same: he couldn't help. It had to stop somewhere.

"Sounds to me like a lame excuse."

"Think what you want."

"I wouldn't mind seeing what all this talk about cutting horses is really all about."

"You just said there are times I might choose not to take Otis into a particular place. I don't want to take him there."

She smirked. "I was talking about someplace really

distracting, like a rock concert where he might have trouble hearing you or people might mistakenly step on his paws. You live on a ranch. Otis has to get accustomed to being around other animals. This is probably a good way to introduce him without having him get overwhelmed."

Cody's head dipped for a second, thinking. And then he nodded. "I'd prefer not to stay long."

Sweet victory! Smiling, Lyssa said, "That's fair enough."

They entered the arena just as Beau eased one of the quarter horses he was training into the herd of cattle. He simply blended among them, pulling them apart as the horse moved until the one cow was chosen. Dusty Dan went head to head with the cow, matching every turn until he was pulled far away from the herd.

Beau had explained at lunch that cutting was a part of ranching and had been for hundreds of years. A good cowboy needed an expert cutting horse to sort through the cattle and separate the ones that needed vaccines or ones being sold at market. During the middle of the century it had become a sport for those cowboys with expert horses who wanted to compete and show off their skills.

Lyssa couldn't fathom how Beau managed to stay on the horse so effortlessly. With each lightning-quick stop, she held her breath, thinking he'd fly over the horse's head. But he held on, and in the blink of an eye, horse and cow changed directions until it seemed the cow was cornered, and just stopped.

Mesmerized, Lyssa hadn't realized her jaw had fallen open until the flying dust settled on her lips and in her mouth. She smacked her lips to rid herself of the taste.

"Glad you made it out here. I could use you this weekend in Fort Worth," Beau said.

Cody tried not to wince. Beau was riding Sassy this weekend, as was right. How else would she get exposure?

"I'm busy."

"It won't take the whole weekend."

"I need to train with Otis."

"Actually, going to Fort Worth would be perfect," Lyssa said, chiming in. "By the weekend the two of you will be settled with each other enough around the ranch and it'll be time to try interacting in public."

"The show is at the Coliseum. It'll be too distracting with all those horses and cows around," Cody argued.

"If he's too distracted by the goings-on at the show, then you'll know it may not be a good idea to take him again. But you're never going to know until you try. You can't shy away from what you do."

"I'm not ready."

"How do you know? Even I can see how you and Otis have taken to each other."

"I'm not talking about the dog." With a heavy sigh, Cody turned and took a few steps away.

Cody started to walk away, his intention simply to end the conversation that had his stomach turning in knots. His mistake, he quickly realized, was letting go of Otis' leash. Abruptly, he stopped walking. He whistled once, but Otis remained seated where he was.

"Come here, Otis," he called. Otis was by his side in an instant. He gripped the dog's leash and relief flooded him.

It was all a roller coaster ride, Cody thought. All his emotions were jumbled up, flying high one moment, and plummeting the next. He hated it.

For a brief moment, fear had clutched him. He'd walked away from Otis and into oblivion. At least, that was the way it always felt when he had no bearing on where he was.

But then he called for the dog and Otis was there, safe and sure by his left leg, waiting to take Cody's command. And the roller coaster leveled out once again.

He could walk away. That easily. As long as Otis was by his side. It was an incredible comfort. Freeing in a way he hadn't felt freedom in months. He didn't have to worry about disappointment or expectations. Dogs weren't like that. They loved unconditionally in a way people didn't.

He could just walk away.

And so he did walk away. And no one followed him. No one hovered around him, waiting to take his arm and move him in the right direction. God, this was the first real peace he'd felt in months.

That was completely true, he decided as he made his way out of the arena. When he was with Lyssa, things were different, comforting. Nothing had changed except for the fact that inside, he felt more like the man he used to be instead of the man he'd hated becoming. But now, even without her, he felt himself coming back.

Lyssa was right. No, he'd never get his life as he knew it back. Not unless this next corneal transplant was a success. And he was banking heavy on it being a success. But he could do something, anything, again with his life. He just had to figure out what he wanted to do that would make him feel as good as working with his cutting horses.

Right now, all he wanted to do was get the heck out of there.

Chapter Six

It hadn't taken but a minute for Cody to decide he was being an idiot and to turn around. He wouldn't let stubbornness get to him this time, not after coming this far.

"Halt, Otis," he said, stopping on the gravel path. He listened for footsteps, for that adorable little growl Lyssa made whenever he did something that ticked her off.

But there was nothing. No one was following him. There were no footsteps on the ground chasing him to make sure he didn't collide with something dangerous he couldn't see.

"Let's go back, Otis." The dog didn't move. "About, Otis."

Otis turned them both around and they proceeded back to the arena. When he walked into the building, he heard Beau and Lyssa talking. Their voices were low, as if they meant to keep their conversation from him, which annoyed him to no end. But he knew that had to be the case.

"What time?" he ground out.

He could hear the surprise in Lyssa's voice. "You came back?"

"Obviously," Cody said, his irritation flaring.

So be it. He wasn't going to pretend he liked their quiet whispers. He was blind, but his hearing was just fine. More than fine, in fact. He could ignore their whispers of worry or he could stand like a man and let them know he was done with it.

It felt real good to stand.

"What time?" he ground out again.

"We need to leave at dawn if we're going to make it to Fort Worth with time to spare."

Cody nodded. It didn't really matter what time or when they were leaving. Or even how long they were staying. It wasn't as if there was a list of chores he had to do before leaving. Those had been divided up and given to hands. Beau had been given his most prided chore. Although, working with his horses had never been a chore to Cody.

He began to walk away and then turned back. "You will be coming with us, Lyssa, won't you?"

"Of course," she said.

"Good."

"We can take my truck," Beau said.

Cody clamped down the sudden irritation running under the surface of his skin, deciding it was irrational. Riding together with Beau would give Cody a chance to get up to speed on what had been happening since he'd been away from the sport.

"That sounds like a good plan."

He headed back to the house with Otis by his left side, still annoyed that his big brother just killed any chance of him getting Lyssa alone this weekend.

Darn big brothers.

* * *

Lyssa didn't want to question the reasons for Cody's about-face. She just decided that victory was sweet and the biggest victory of all would be Cody's in the end. She thanked Beau and then headed out of the arena in search of Cody.

He'd retreated quickly, not bothering to ask if she wanted to come with him. Instead of feeling slighted, she chose to take that as a good sign that Cody was finally seeing his independence again.

She caught up with them as they were climbing the front porch steps.

"I was a little nervous about picking a dog for you without having met you first. But after watching you work together these past few days I see that Otis was the perfect choice for you," she said in admiration.

Otis was a tall dog and matched perfectly with Cody's height and arm extension. He responded well to the deep timbre of Cody's voice. Otis' first handler had been elderly. They'd been together for two years before his handler suffered a fatal stroke. Otis had stayed by his side for two days until he was found.

When Otis was brought back to the school, he appeared to be depressed, his spirit broken in a way that tore at Lyssa's heart. She'd recognized that same torn spirit in Cody when she'd first arrived. Otis was a proud dog and seeing him work with Cody was enough to convince Lyssa that choosing Otis for Cody had been the right move.

They walked through the door and Cody immediately put his right arm out to feel his way through the room.

"After a while, you'll become more comfortable with Otis walking through the room and giving you enough clearance so you won't bump into anything. You won't feel the need to extend your hand for guidance."

"Something smells good. It must be time for dinner. Or close to it."

Lyssa had ignored the rumble of her own stomach because training had been going so well. But now that the aroma of good food assaulted her, her hunger pangs began to grow stronger.

"I understand the need to take Otis with me pretty much everywhere I go. But what about on a date?"

She was thrown by his question, although she couldn't figure out why. It was a perfectly normal question that she'd answered hundreds of times for her students.

"Of course, if that's what you want. Again, it's your choice."

"You mean he won't climb up on the sofa and snuggle up between me and my date?"

Lyssa's insides suddenly burned. Since that first day in the field, when she'd thought Cody was about to kiss her, they'd danced around something, but always stopped short of any confession. Getting involved with a student in any way other than professionally wouldn't be right. But hearing Cody talking about dating turned her an ugly shade of green. Instead of letting the sudden pang of jealousy get the best of her, she gave the standard answer.

"He'll stay by your side. You can snuggle with whomever you please and he'll behave properly. He's trained not to go on furniture. He's very well-mannered, so you don't have to worry about him not behaving when you take him to someone else's home.

He'll stay by your side and sit by you, even by the dinner table. He won't beg for food."

"Really? So he's my shadow from now on."

"More like your eyes and your best friend."

Cody nodded, his lips just short of a smile, Lyssa noticed.

"Do you like to dance?"

The abrupt change in subject caught Lyssa off guard once again. "Excuse me?"

"Dancing. You know, to music. I used to take my dates dancing all the time. There is a great dance hall a few towns from here."

"I don't dance very well."

She coughed and shifted in place, trying to shake out this green-eyed envy piercing her. Going to a weekend cutting horse competition was one thing. Tagging along on one of Cody's dates was totally . . . it just wasn't happening. Period.

She struggled, trying to force some professionalism into her voice. This wasn't about her. It was about Cody.

"Getting out in a public place is a great next step. Maybe trying something smaller before Saturday would be a good idea."

He flashed a quick smile that had her catching her breath and made her knees weak. "Good," he said.

"But I don't really think my coming on one of your dates is appropriate. This could be a test run for you and maybe—"

She stopped mid-sentence, taking in the tilt of his jaw and the devilish amusement playing at the corner of his lips. He was smiling one of those wide grins that showed how perfectly straight his teeth were and how adorable a man with dimpled cheeks could be.

He knew she was flustered. And darn him, he was enjoying every second of it.

His voice was low and slightly gruff when he spoke. "I wasn't asking if you wanted to come on my date with me, Lyssa. I was asking you to be my date."

Her heart did a flip. And she felt like an idiot. "Oh."

"Is that a problem? I mean, with the school? Is there some handbook rule that prevents you from going dancing with me?"

She chuckled, more with relief than anything. "The only rule is the law of coordination—in that I don't have any. You do remember the incident by the pool, don't you?"

She fought the scorching blush, but it came anyway, blistering her cheeks until she dipped her head, averting her gaze. Even knowing Cody couldn't see it didn't help.

"I can help you with that."

A nervous laugh escaped her lips before she could catch it. "Believe me. Many a man has tried and found it to be a lost cause." Okay, so maybe the many men consisted only of her father and Chad, but that was enough humiliation for her.

"They're not me."

A cocky remark. One that she was sure came straight from the core.

Her heart hammered. "I don't have anything appropriate to wear."

"You're full of excuses. It's not a black tie affair, Lyssa. It's just some club with some good country music. Brock mentioned at breakfast he'd be playing there tonight. I haven't been out to see him play in a while and I'm sure he'll be happy someone finally dragged me out of the house. Not to mention having a little family support of his own for a change."

Lyssa didn't know much about the two youngest Gentry men, but she'd heard bits and pieces at the dinner table. Jackson, next in line after Cody, had yet to make an appearance at the ranch. From what little Cody had said about him, she knew only that he was in law enforcement.

Brock, the youngest of the brothers, was as scarce around the house as Jackson, although technically he did still live there. He was a musician from the cradle, Cody had said. Every once in a while she'd hear the mellow sound of a guitar playing down the hall, and the haunting voice of a man singing of lost love. She knew it was Brock, but the way he'd hole up in his room, Lyssa thought he was more of a phantom.

She knew Cody didn't think much of Brock's choice to pursue fame and fortune in country music. She knew Mike Gentry approved of it even less. But at least Cody supported it because he knew it mattered to Brock.

"I don't know," she said, nibbling on her bottom lip.

"If you're nervous about us going alone, we can always ask Beau and Mandy if they'd like to come."

"Sure, more people to witness my fine dancing performance."

She sighed. She was really being ridiculous. There was nothing saying her time at the ranch had to be all work and no play. With Beau and Mandy tagging along it wouldn't really be a date. It'd just be a bunch of people together.

"I guess. Okay."

"Good. And don't worry about the clothes. Anything you have will fit in just fine where we're headed."

As Cody had mentioned, Brock's reaction to having him go to one of his gigs was met with much enthusiasm. Their father regarded the youngest boy's musical aspirations as nothing more than a fleeting fancy and discouraged him at every turn.

But Lyssa had had a chance to listen through closed doors to the haunting words and music Cody's brother created. He had talent. She didn't need to know anything about music to appreciate it. And the fact that Cody not only recognized that talent but acknowledged it had brought a lot of satisfaction to Brock at the dinner table that evening.

Later, when Lyssa was plowing through what little she'd packed to come to the ranch, she tried to convince herself that tonight's trek out to see Brock play wasn't really a date. As she yanked a skirt out of the closet and tried to find a matching blouse from the drawer she continued building the illusion. This wasn't a date. It was merely a public test run, much like the ones she went on with all her students.

She'd exhausted all combinations of jeans, skirts, and blouses, until she finally decided that none of it mattered. Cody couldn't see what she was wearing, only she could. It wouldn't really matter to anyone else anyway.

She finally slipped into a cotton sundress that she realized with dismay looked like a potato sack over her slightly pear-shaped figure. A low pair of white leather sandals and a touch of makeup was all she'd allow herself to fuss with for this evening. Tossing the dress in her bag had been a last-minute whim, but now she was glad she'd had some semblance of foresight to pack it. The only other things she had were clothes she wore when working with the dogs.

She met Cody downstairs in the living room. The house was quiet except for the slap of her sandals against the heels of her feet. Cody rose up from the sofa when she walked into the room.

His colorful western shirt was pressed neatly, most likely by Isadore, as was the seemingly new pair of Wranglers he wore. His boots were polished to a shine and the straw hat on his head looked as if it were his Sunday best.

"You look beautiful," he said.

She smirked. "How would you know?"

"Because I just heard Isadore sigh in the other room when she saw you coming down the stairs, so she must approve. And that's saying something for Isadore." He leaned forward slightly and whispered just below his normal tone, but loud enough to be heard by anyone who was inclined to eavesdrop. "She's watching, even if she doesn't want me to know."

Lyssa heard the sound of what was probably a broom or mop hitting the inside of the pantry.

"See what I mean?" he said, laughing.

"You look nice and it makes me feel a little under-dressed."

"Don't worry about it." He sighed. "I wish I could see you."

Lyssa dipped her head. How did he always do that? How did he always manage to make her feel as if she were the most beautiful woman in the world?

She reached out and lifted his hand to her face. Lightly, he ran his fingers over her newly painted lips and then cupped her cheek. It brought a smile to his face and one to her heart.

"Brock left right after dinner. He had to set up early and do a sound check before everyone arrives at the club."

"Are we picking up Beau and Mandy or are they meeting us here?"

"Ah, they aren't coming. When I called the ranch, Mandy said Beau was wiped out, not that I blame him. He's been doing double duty here and at the Double T. Little Promise has an ear infection, so they're going to sit this one out. It's just you and me."

He extended his left arm for her to hook her own through.

"Right."

Cody stopped short. "No seriously. I asked, but they begged off."

Lyssa shook her head. "Give me your right arm. Use your left hand for Otis," she corrected. "Speaking of Otis, where is he?"

"Oh, I forgot."

"After a while you won't. It will become second nature."

"What I mean is I've decided not to take Otis tonight. He's upstairs in my bedroom."

She frowned. "Why?"

"I'd like to try this first outing alone."

Knotting her arms in front of her chest, Lyssa said, "What are you going to do when you have to go to the men's room?"

Cody smiled devilishly. "I'll hold it."

She rolled her eyes. "I thought the whole point in going was to get you out in public with Otis?"

"Maybe to you."

"Oh, really. What was your purpose then?"

"Do you really have to ask?"

"As a matter of fact, yes, I do. I can never figure you out, Cody, and just when I think I have, you do something like say you want to leave Otis home when my whole reason for being here in the first place is to help the two of you bond and become best buddies."

He smiled. "If it's all the same to you, tonight I'd rather become your best buddy. If he's going to be sleeping with me later, then we'll have all the bonding time in the world. I don't need him snuggling in between the two of us all night long."

Lyssa stared wordlessly at him, her heart pounding as she fought the image that sprang to mind of the two of them locked in a tight embrace.

"Don't you dare ruin my dog, Cody Gentry," she managed to say after a few moments. "He will not be sleeping with you."

"I thought you said he was my dog."

Lyssa shrugged. "He's never going to stop being my dog, no matter how long he's here on the ranch. And I will not have you undo all the training that's made him a good guide dog."

"I'll behave."

"You'd better."

"Or what?"

"You're impossible."

The look on his face told her she was as big a wimp as she felt.

"Okay, he can stay home this once," she conceded. "But not this weekend. We're taking him to Fort Worth."

"The Coliseum can get pretty crowded," he warned.

"This is what you do, Cody. Otis needs to get exposure in the places you go frequently. You can't keep him home all the time, or what's the point in having him?"

His eyebrows raised beneath his sunglasses. She knew he was thinking about the fact that he hadn't been the one who wanted a guide dog in the first place. It had been forced on him from the beginning, first by his father and then by Lyssa.

She sighed. "He stays home tonight, but he goes to Fort Worth."

"I'll agree to that."

Cody reached into his pocket and extracted a set of keys on a leather strap.

"You don't mind driving, do you? I mean, I usually take the Mercedes when I take a lady out, but it's been sitting idle these last months collecting dust."

Lyssa's eyebrow rose in interest. "You want me to drive your Mercedes?"

"Yeah, Brock will probably be ticked off since he's the only one who's been driving it lately, but he'll get over it."

She smiled. A Mercedes. It sounded like fun.

The Dance Hall was more crowded than Lyssa anticipated it would be on a Wednesday evening. It had been fun driving the Mercedes out on the open road, but now that she was faced with parking an elegant car like this in a pot-hole-filled parking lot with cars jammed into every inch of available space, she was starting to sweat. Her stomach jumped as she navigated the car through narrow passages. Beads of sweat sprung out on her forehead. She blew a quick breath of air upward to cool herself down.

"Relax, you can't possibly do any more damage

than Brock," Cody had said in response to the little murmur of distress she made when she stopped at the entrance to the parking lot.

"Want to bet?" she'd said.

And he had just laughed, making her nerves all the more jumpy.

Why in the heck was she so nervous, anyway? It wasn't just the car. And it wasn't as if she hadn't been out on a date before.

Her hands trembled on the steering wheel as she saw a couple walking arm in arm into the dance hall.

This isn't a date, she told herself. But suddenly Lyssa realized with dread that a date was exactly what this was. She was on a date with Cody. Otis was home. She wasn't in the company of any family members. It was just her and Cody, now walking arm in arm toward the dance hall just like the other couple she'd seen as she parked the Mercedes.

Oh, this evening was shaping up just perfectly.

For most of the night, they sat in a corner table close enough to the stage for Brock to bounce back and forth between their table and a table where some of his friends were gathered. Another band went on stage before his band.

The music was too loud for Lyssa's liking. That plus sitting too close to the PA system made it difficult to follow the conversation among the other people who stopped by their table.

Cody didn't say much. He mostly listened, leaning back in his chair with his arm draped casually over the back of hers, making it clear that they were together. As if they were a couple. And thinking about Cody that way, allowing herself to think of him purely as a man and not a student, was something that made Lyssa uneasy.

As usual, Cody kept his sunglasses on while inside, most likely to hide his eyes. And as they sat in the loud room among all the other people, Lyssa wondered about Cody's eyes. What they'd been like before the accident.

There were pictures, of course, scattered around the house, showing the various stages of growth of all the Gentry boys. All the brothers had light eyes. Cody's, though, had intrigued Lyssa from the start. In some pictures, they'd been a mixture of blue and green. Sometimes, when the sun was shining bright, they'd appeared a deep green. Other times, they were almost a dark blue.

Besides their color, Lyssa couldn't help but wonder what she'd see if she looked into Cody's eyes while he was looking back at her. Really seeing her. The thought made her catch her breath.

Cody glanced around the room as if he could see what was going on. In truth, it was a natural reaction to the sound around him. Voices maybe. As Lyssa scanned the room herself she saw more than a few women glancing in their direction, some overtly sizing *her* up and coming out a little smug.

"You've been hiding yourself out."

Lyssa glanced up to find one of the women she'd seen earlier scrutinizing them in the corner had finally sidled up next to Cody. She was rubbing Cody's arm up and down and practically inviting herself into his lap. The blue jeans she wore were snug enough to be a second skin, as was the red cotton shirt she wore.

Lyssa squashed down the sudden stab of jealousy that leveled her.

Cody's grip tightened on the table. His voice seemed forced when he spoke. "Haven't felt like dancing much lately. How are you, Susan?"

"Fine. Just fine. I hope you'll be in the mood for some dancing tonight though. Brock usually sets this place on fire, but maybe we can convince your baby brother to put a slow number or two on his setlist. You be sure to save a dance for me, won't you now?"

She'd actually purred, Lyssa thought. Was she for real or what?

Petty. Don't go getting petty, Lyssa, she admonished herself.

"Sorry, Susan. My dance card is filled for the evening."

"Oh, don't break my heart," Susan said in a soft whine.

"Susan, this is Lyssa McEl . . . Geez, I never get your name right."

"McElhannon," Lyssa said, extending her hand in greeting.

Awkwardly, the two women shook hands. Susan's smile was forced, even seemed a little unsure.

Susan cocked her head to one side, her blond mane framing her face, and pasted a saccharin-sweet smile on her face. "You two been together long?"

It wasn't so much the question that threw Lyssa, but the bluntness of it. While she tried to find her voice, Cody answered.

"Lyssa's staying at the ranch."

Susan gave her a pointed glance, making her wonder just what kind of relationship she and Cody had shared before he'd lost his vision. No, she wouldn't go there. It was none of her business.

"Really? You must be loving it then, Lyssa. The

trails through the ranch are beautiful. Cody knows just how to show you right."

They were loaded words Lyssa knew she was wise to ignore.

"Susan's a veterinarian, Lyssa. She's been out to the ranch quite a few times over the past few years when we've been in need."

Susan smiled with pride, as if that one bit of information Cody had revealed gave her the upper hand. Lyssa wanted to say there wasn't any reason for winning any hand where Cody was concerned. But the play of woman against woman was as old as time.

"In what capacity are you at the ranch?"

Cody laughed so hard it stopped the conversation between Brock and one of his backup singers, a girl named Cheryl, who was seated at the next table.

"She's my trainer," Cody said easily. But there was a tightness about him that suddenly made Lyssa think he wasn't enjoying this interplay as much as he let on.

"I train guide dogs," Lyssa offered, looking at Cody, trying to read the emotions changing on his face.

"Oh, well, that's right. I knew about the accident, of course, but I thought . . ."

"I haven't hidden so much from the world that the people around me don't know I'm blind. Besides, word gets around."

"I'm sorry, Cody. Brock mentioned some surgery you were having not long ago."

"Yeah, it didn't work." There was only a tinge of regret in his voice, but Lyssa knew it ran much deeper.

Brock got up from the table and climbed to the stage.

As if it were her cue, Susan said, "Well, I guess your brother is getting ready for his set."

"I guess so."

"It was good seeing ... I'll be stopping by real soon."

Cody didn't look in Susan's direction as she walked away, her boot heels clinking on the shiny boards of the dance floor.

"She's a beautiful woman."

"Yes, she is."

"There's no reason for you not to dance—"

"Geez, Lys, you are so darned irritating sometimes," Cody said, reaching out and searching for her hand. He sighed. "I'm with you tonight. I'm not some good-for-nothing jerk who's going to go off dancing with every other woman in the dance hall just because they asked. I asked you to come tonight so I could get you in my arms, and that's exactly what I intend to do."

"You don't have to be so pushy about it."

His chuckle seemed to come from deep in his soul. "With you, lady, I most certainly do. Now let's dance."

Chapter Seven

"Don't act as if I haven't made my intentions to-night plain, Lyssa," Cody said, the deep timbre of his voice leaving Lyssa weak in the knees. "I kind of fig-ured you wouldn't be too receptive to me pulling you into my arms back at the ranch. Chances are someone would be around to witness it. Isadore, most likely. You strike me as the shy type where embracing is concerned."

He wanted to hold her. This wasn't just some outing to test his boundaries. She closed her eyes at the thought of being in Cody's embrace, feeling muscled arms that she knew were strong and reassuring.

"I'm not shy," she said, swallowing the sudden lump stuck tight in her throat.

He nodded once. "Good, because I plan on getting the chance to hold you a lot tonight. For starters, right here on this dance floor."

"Do I have a say in any of this?"

"I figure you had your say back at the ranch when you decided to come."

He was smiling, something potent and telling. As if he could see just how flustered she was and was enjoying every bit of it.

She jut out her chin ever so slightly. "What about Susan?"

His brow knitted. "What about her?"

"She might have a thing or two to say about it."

"I couldn't imagine why."

It was her turn to laugh. "Oh, come on, Cody. The woman is so totally over the moon for you. I didn't have to look that hard to see it."

"Over the moon, huh?"

"That's right."

It was hard to tell if the slight irritation that was crawling just below the surface of her skin was also evident in her tone of voice. It wasn't very attractive to see and it certainly wasn't something Lyssa enjoyed feeling.

Cody leaned closer, dipping his head, and she could tell that he was a little unsure by the slight catch in his voice when he spoke. That put them on even ground.

"In case you haven't noticed, I'm pretty close to being over the moon for you. And obviously I'm not doing this right because if I were, we wouldn't be standing here discussing moons. You'd already be snug up close."

Her head was swimming and she had to catch her breath.

"So what do you say?"

He extended his arm just as Brock announced the band and began their first number. The crowd was full of fire and jumped to their feet.

For God's sake, what was she so afraid of? It wasn't

like she'd never gone dancing in her whole life. She'd just never gone dancing with Cody.

It wasn't fear of making a fool of herself on the dance floor. There she had no trouble feeling comfortable, even knowing she had the grace of a duck. It was being a fool of another kind that kept making her act like an idiot.

They'd misstepped a few times, Cody leading her and the rest of the crowd seeming to part to allow them room to move. The fast song ended and Brock immediately slipped into a slower number. From the first few strums of the guitar, Lyssa recognized it as one of the songs she'd heard Brock playing in his bedroom.

Somehow, Cody had hooked his arm around her waist and drawn her closer to him without Lyssa realizing it. The close proximity forced her to see things she hadn't allowed herself to see before. Being in Cody's arms made her aware of him on a completely new level. She'd known he was tall and strong, with an edge of control that allowed him to keep his feelings at bay. But he was gentle, too. And that surprised Lyssa. The warmth of his body fused with her heat and the light scent of her perfume mingled with the muskiness of his cologne.

Her head was turned to one side as they danced. Cody dipped his head and brushed his smoothly shaven cheek against hers. With trembling hands, she clung to his shoulders.

"You've never been kissed?" he whispered, his hot breath tickling her ear.

"Don't be ridiculous. Of course I have."

Her cheeks flamed just thinking about it. About

kissing Cody. As if he'd known all along that was exactly what had been on her mind.

Sure, she had been kissed, but she was almost certain Cody wasn't talking about the sweet good-night kisses she'd had with the dates she rarely went on.

"Then why are you trembling?"

She closed her eyes. "I'm not."

"My senses are—"

"I know, because you've lost the use of your eyes your other senses have sharpened. I'm just cold."

"I can remedy that." He pulled her closer so that she was completely enveloped in his warmth and her head spun.

A rumble of laughter escaped his lips. "Okay, so you've been kissed. But you've never been kissed by a man."

Rolling her eyes, Lyssa said, "I'll be sure to tell Chad that the next time I see him."

Cody stopped dancing, and his arms went rigid. "Chad. Who's that?"

Lyssa had walked right into that one with blinders on. She'd been quick to prove Cody wrong, but in mentioning Chad, she most surely would only strengthen his case. And Cody wasn't likely to let her slip pass.

"An ex-boyfriend."

He nodded and began dancing again. "Some fleeting moment in time?"

"Actually, we dated for over a year the first year I worked at the school."

"I want to punch the guy, but I'll thank him instead for being stupid enough to let you go."

A pain of regret stabbed her heart and had her closing her eyes again. "He was my first instructor when I learned to train guide dogs."

"And you dated him."

"Yes."

"I'll bet he kissed like a fish."

A soft giggle escaped Lyssa's lips before she could hold it back. She could have described Chad that way herself if it hadn't hurt so much. She knew the reason why kissing Chad wasn't anything special was because there simply was no passion in him. Not for her, anyway.

"You don't know what you're talking about."

"No? If you'd been with a man for a year and he'd kissed you proper, having me hold you like this wouldn't affect you the way it does."

"And how's that?"

"You want to bolt from my arms. You could, you know. I couldn't chase after you if you did. I don't have Otis to help me sniff you out."

He smiled, as if he'd anticipated her blush.

"But there's this part of you that wants to stay and know what it is like for me to kiss you. If you'd been kissed—I mean *really* kissed—you'd know. And your reaction to me would be different."

She sighed softly. "Is that so shocking?"

"Yes. I can't imagine a man alive who wouldn't dream of holding you like this and kissing you. Anyone who'd let you go is an idiot. So what happened with you and this Chad anyway?"

"I thought his loss was your gain? Why would you care?" She stepped on his boot as they turned, wincing, but Cody did nothing to acknowledge her blunder.

He shrugged. "Curious."

"Maybe it's because I have two left feet. I mean,

how can you be this good at this? I can see what I'm doing and I'm stepping all over you."

"You're doing fine."

"Because you're dragging me with you."

Cody reached his hand up and ran his fingers lightly down her face. "Close your eyes."

"No, it's taken me too long to get my sight, I don't want to shut anything out."

He chuckled. "Lyssa, just cooperate and close your eyes."

She did so and his hands cupped her face. As his lips moved over hers the ground beneath her seemed to swell and her body swayed. It wasn't the sweet kiss she had initially expected. But somewhere deep down, she *had* expected it.

Telling herself over and over again as she dressed earlier that this wasn't a date had been denial in the biggest form. Cody had made his intentions crystal clear. She'd known right from the start that this was exactly what she'd wanted to happen tonight, too. Right down to the moment she'd chosen this simple sundress that made her feel as feminine as the lacy underthings she wore.

Cody could see none of that. And still, he was kissing her, making her feel these incredible feelings, reaching an untouched place in her soul.

The kiss was slow and meaningful. His lips lingered on hers and she was in no hurry for that to change. The scent of him enveloped her, filling her head and touching all of her senses. His fingers were in her hair, stroking lightly, exploring as carefully as his mouth was.

And then the music stopped. Lyssa opened her eyes

and realized they were standing still. Everyone else had moved off the dance floor.

"The music stopped, Cody."

"Did it?"

"People are . . . staring at us?"

"Really? I can't see that."

She giggled, gazing up at him and seeing his lips stretch into a smile. The music started again. "You want to keep dragging me across the floor?"

"If it will keep you in my arms, I'll do it all night."

"How can you dance like this and not see where you're going?"

"Some things you can do just fine with your eyes closed. Like kissing." He bent his head. This time she met him halfway.

Against every will she had, she trembled in his arms, confirming everything he'd said a few minutes ago. He put one hand on the nape of her neck and cupped her cheek with the other, his thumb brushing her lips. And then he kissed her again.

It amazed Lyssa that she didn't pull back. Not this time. For most of her life she'd played things by the rules, pulled back when unsure, plunged in when she knew things were right. Took care and didn't take chances.

Somewhere deep inside, as Cody slipped his hand lower on her waist and drew her closer to him still, warning bells clanged in a warning she would have heeded at one time, but now chose to ignore.

Cody wasn't Chad, he was Cody. He was with her because . . .

Because she'd forced herself into his life when he'd become unreachable.

Lyssa didn't want to think this was a simple case

of Florence Nightingale syndrome. Lyssa hadn't saved Cody. She certainly wasn't his lifeline. But the danger of that was too great.

"What are you so afraid of?" he whispered as he drew back.

"I don't . . . know what you're talking about."

"Sure you do. You always do, it seems. You were right with me and now . . . I don't know, you're holding back."

"Am I?" Playing dumb didn't make her feel any better.

"Does kissing in public embarrass you?"

Her shoulders sagged. "Why are you making a big deal of this?"

He took a step back, but still held her upper arm. His voice grew deeper as he spoke. "Because it is. I don't want you to feel embarrassed."

Awareness of what he was implying flooded her. "My God, Cody, it's not you," she said resolutely. "This isn't about you."

"Darlin', in my arms like this, kissing me the way we were kissing, I figure it's most definitely about me to some degree if you're suddenly pulling back."

Before Lyssa could even think, she took a step closer, into his arms, settling her head on his shoulder. It was irrational for her to hide from Cody's gaze. He couldn't see her. But suddenly, she wanted to be invisible to him, if only to hide the feelings of doubt consuming her now.

"Please tell me what's wrong, Lyssa."

"Nothing."

"Don't give me that."

"You pegged me good, Cody," she said, trying to

keep her voice light. "You're not the only one with fears."

He lifted his hand, found her cheek on the first attempt and cupped it. "I'm sorry."

"Don't apologize."

"I wasn't thinking. I made you feel uncomfortable."

"I told you it isn't about you."

"Then what is it?"

She wanted to both laugh and cry. How could she put into words all the crazy feelings raging inside her? She was confident about what she knew. She was good at what she did at the school. Beyond that, life scared her. Holding Cody like this terrified her. How crazy was that?

He's just a man, she told herself. Flesh and blood. She couldn't find the right words to tell him being here like this with him was making her want to run and hide. It made her think of things she'd never thought existed in her.

Lyssa didn't know how to rise above her consuming feelings of fear and self-doubt. And she didn't want to hide in this shadow that was between her and Cody. She wanted to trust that what was happening between them was something real.

"Let's just say, there are some things I'm not. And some things I'm not very sure of. Please don't ask anymore."

To her great relief, Cody didn't push the issue any further. He just led her off the dance floor. And she knew for a fact that he was somehow the one still leading because she found herself back at the table and lifting her drink to her lips before she could even fathom how she'd gotten there.

Lyssa struggled through the rest of the evening, trying to push aside the feeling of longing, the memory of being in Cody's arms, the sexy smile on his face that made her feel like she was the most beautiful woman in the world.

She liked the feeling, liked even more that he seemed to share that feeling. And for once that was comforting.

Still, for every time she felt her head swim, she'd held herself back. She was playing with fire. She wasn't staying. She definitely wouldn't allow herself to do something stupid like fall in love, like she had with Chad. But she feared it was already too late.

They drove back to the ranch in silence. Wondering what Cody was thinking was killing her. He'd seen right through her tonight in a way that was startling, chipping away at the lock that chained her fears.

Isadore was most likely settled in her room, which was comforting. Lyssa already knew the normal household routine. Cody walked through the front door behind her and locked it. Whether he knew it or not, he was growing more comfortable moving through the house even without Otis. That was a comforting thought. Her time here was worth it, but it wasn't going to last.

Her chest tightened at the thought. It was inevitable that she would leave and go back to working at the school. Other students needed her experience. And the money Mike Gentry had gifted the school would go a long way toward helping those students.

That's where she belonged, not on a ranch in the middle of nowhere.

Yes, there were possibilities out there beyond what she knew and felt comfortable with. Maybe she was getting a little too comfortable in her own skin, as

Cody had said. Maybe she did need to stretch herself and find out what she could become. But it wasn't out of fear, as he'd suggested. Right now her biggest fear was that everything they'd shared tonight was an illusion.

They reached the landing at the top of the stairs and walked side by side over wide wooden planked floors. They reached her bedroom door first.

"Good night, Cody," she said softly, although she knew she didn't need to keep her voice down for anyone. There wasn't anyone there to disturb. But there was something about quiet steps in the night.

"Lyssa?"

He'd stopped next to her. She kept her hand on the door, fighting the urgent sense to bolt through the door and lock herself inside her bedroom. Cody had already seen way more than she wanted him to.

"What is it?"

He inched closer and she didn't know what she feared more, that Cody would kiss her again or that he wouldn't.

He didn't kiss her.

She wasn't at all surprised at the tumble of her heart. It was completely irrational for her to feel that way, but she couldn't help it.

"I may not be able to see my hand in front of my face, but I see you, Lyssa. And I like very much what I see. All those fears you've got locked up inside yourself, they only matter to you. You don't have to hide them from me."

"You're suddenly so sure of everything about me, Cody?"

She tried to keep her voice light, tried to deny he

wasn't dead on center about all those things she'd struggled against tonight. But it was no use.

As scary as it was, it was also comforting. To be able to let her hair down and allow someone access to all those secrets in her soul was freeing.

"No," Cody said, lifting his hand and resting it on the doorjamb, just above her head. "There's a whole lot I'm not sure of. A whole lot more I don't know. But I'm anxious to learn."

He smiled then, and her head began to swim. Did he have any idea of the effect that perfect smile had on her peace of mind?

"Good night, Cody," she whispered.

Reaching up on her toes, she placed both hands on either side of his face and pressed her mouth to his. She'd intended it to be a simple kiss, one that would be the perfect ending to the evening they'd shared. But to Lyssa's amazement, it quickly became much more.

With one swift movement and a harsh intake of breath Cody dragged Lyssa against him, wrapping his arms around her waist. In his arms, she trembled, feeling herself go weak. His mouth was hungry, demanding a response that she readily gave, wanting to share. Their bodies seem to meld together as their kiss deepened, leaving her soul raw and exposed.

Lyssa's mind was still reeling from the explosion of sensation coursing through her when Cody pulled away.

Tipping his hat just a fraction, he whispered, "Night, Lyssa."

With one hand, she felt for the door, realized it was open, and walked backward into the room, closing the door behind her. She leaned her back against the door with her cheek against the smooth, cool wood, listening to the hammer of her pulse against her eardrum, listening to the smooth steps of Cody's boots as he made his way down the hallway toward his bedroom.

The door opened, then closed, and she was left with nothing but the sound of her heartbeat pounding against the walls of her chest.

She pounded her head on the door with frustration. *You idiot*, she thought. *Don't be a fool and fall in love with this man.*

But it was already too late.

Chapter Eight

"Who's going to be there?" Lyssa asked. "I mean, are they all cowboys like you? You know, people who have ranches."

"You'll see a lot of weekenders at shows. There's usually plenty of those."

"Weekenders. What's that?"

"Weekenders are people with regular day jobs who just love the sport of cuttin'. They head out on the weekends to whatever events they can to try to win some money and have a good time. It's not just the cowboys, either. Plenty of women are real good and can put me to shame, even on my best day."

That had to be saying something, because from what Beau had told Lyssa that morning before they'd climbed into the truck to leave for Fort Worth, Cody didn't have bad days. He was that good. The championship titles he'd won spoke of his skill, and the reputation of his work with horses had people coming from all over the country in the hopes that they could train with the best.

Things had changed between them. They were no longer just teacher and student. There was more. Cody had to feel it. How could he not? The kisses they'd shared were . . . electric—mind blowing.

Lyssa's first instinct was to pretend these feelings didn't exist. It was completely inappropriate for her to become involved with Cody. She found her mind wandering to thoughts of him, the way he'd held her in his arms, even when he wasn't there. He could be totally annoying, completely difficult at times.

On the other hand, there'd never been a time in Lyssa's life when she felt so alive. That was a dangerous sign that should have stopped her dead in her tracks.

But denying what was going on between them now wouldn't be fair to either one of them. They were adults. They both knew and understood her reasons for being at the ranch in the first place. There was no harm in enjoying each other's company for the time they had together. She just couldn't lose focus on what she had to accomplish before it was time to leave.

It had helped Lyssa to get some insight into what Cody was fighting against. From what Beau had said, Cody had always been a man driven, and it wasn't always clear what it was chasing his soul. He loved his horses, loved the ranch. He was basically a simple man.

There'd been women, of course, but he'd never stayed with anyone long enough to carve a deep mark. Aside from what he loved that was visible to the world, there was a lot Beau doubted Cody would share with anyone.

Well, maybe not with her, Lyssa decided as she sat in the back seat of the truck with Cody and Otis during the long drive out to Fort Worth. And it didn't really matter anyway, because that wasn't her purpose in coming to this ranch.

Cody had made strides over the few days he'd been working with Otis. Normally, students would stay nearly a month at the school and then they'd return home to fully bond with their new guide dog. She had the month booked and some time after that if needed.

It was going to be a long month. And yet, Lyssa wondered if a month could possibly be enough.

The drive out to Fort Worth was a long one. At least it seemed that way to Cody. There was nothing but music on the radio and Otis warming his feet. The dog sat on the floor in front of him, which normally wouldn't have been a problem if all they were doing was riding across town. But the monotonous two-hour ride was daunting. Cody finally asked Beau to stop to give the poor dog a chance to get up and breathe something other than the scent of his boot leather.

Otis was a good dog, well-mannered and behaved. Lyssa had done right by him and trained him well.

Lyssa had been quiet, not saying much about anything. It may have been because Beau and Mandy were there, chattering to themselves, worried about leaving Promise for the day. But Cody didn't think so.

Things had changed between him and Lyssa. After dancing like they had the other night, kissing her the way he had, Cody knew things had changed a whole lot for him. Sure, the idea of a dog in tow wherever he went wasn't too appealing, but as Lyssa said, he'd probably get used to that after a matter of time. Hopefully, it wouldn't be for too long if his next surgery was successful. For the time being, it would just be him and Otis.

Except, Cody wasn't so sure he wanted *just* Otis in this package. Lyssa had become a warm ray of sunshine in his life. And he hadn't had a slice of sun in a long while.

He could take what was there and forget about what might happen tomorrow. He'd done that the bulk of his life where women were concerned. But tomorrow suddenly seemed too short a time, when only a month ago he was waiting until his eyes healed enough for the next transplant. A month ago, tomorrow couldn't come too soon.

Women. Introduce a stubborn woman into your life and it was a sure way to mess up a man's head.

Cody couldn't help thinking about the feel of Lyssa though, soft and slight. The way she'd gripped his shoulders with hands that felt so strong and so small. The way he'd moved with her. She so unsure of her step and yet willing to let a blind man lead her.

That too had been a welcome change in his life.

He only wished he'd been able to see her face, to look into her eyes when he bent his head and kissed her. Yeah, that he liked. She felt good as she came undone with that kiss. It wasn't just an ego thing. It was more that Cody didn't want to feel that way alone.

Cody relived that night as they made the long drive to Fort Worth. He could almost feel the softness of her curves as she'd melted against him. It had been too long since he'd held a woman in his arms that way, or even cared to, for that matter. Holding Lyssa again, feeling the way her body fit so perfectly against his, was all he could think about. Even now, as he sat next to her and breathed in the faint scent of vanilla, his mind reeled with the memory of holding her close to him.

They'd arrived at the Will Rodgers Coliseum amidst a flurry of activity. Cody let Beau take the lead, getting Sweet Sassy's Smile settled while he moved with Lyssa and Otis into the arena. Beau was the one riding Sassy today. Not Cody.

The raw smell of hay and animal immediately ignited the sense of excitement Cody always felt in competition. The sound of cattle being moved and settled by the herders told him they'd arrived during the middle of a cattle change in the competition.

"You're going to have to tell me what's going on because I've never been to one of these competitions," Lyssa said.

As she spoke, her voice faded slightly, then returned as if she was looking around, trying to take in everything. The Coliseum was huge, but it was the activity, people moving past him, the chatter of cowboys and cowgirls anticipating their ride, that locked onto Cody's mind.

He remembered that feeling well, the anticipation of the ride, the adrenaline rush just when his horse's muscles flexed and then jumped into action.

He swallowed the lump that lodged good and deep in his throat, constricting it like a snake choking the life out of its prey. He missed cutting. What was he thinking when he agreed to come here? He had to be temporarily insane.

Lyssa leaned into him and with the simple reassuring brush of her hand across his back, the feelings consuming him were gone.

It didn't take long for people he knew to come up and offer a greeting. In the end, being among what was natural for him wasn't as hard as Cody had antici- pated. Most of the people he introduced to Lyssa were longtime friends whom he'd backed away from these last months while he adjusted to how his life had changed. There was no pity in their voices. No sense that time had passed at all or that he was any different despite having Otis by his side.

And he was glad, too, that Lyssa was there. For more reasons than one. Having her field the inevitable questions about Otis, hearing how she spoke with such pride, it was hard for Cody to feel anything but lucky to have a guide dog.

But having her there beside him, with him, made all the difference in the world. There was something about hearing the sweet lilt of her voice, having her bend her head intimately close to him, resting her chin on his shoulder so that he could feel her soft breath against his ear when she asked him questions, made his anxiety ease.

He knew the Coliseum from memory. He'd been there often enough. But Cody was amazed at the con- centration it must have taken for Otis to stay focused and lead him through the crowded arena. There were distractions aplenty. He now understood why some handlers would decide to keep their guide dogs away. But a bit of pride tugged at him at how Otis dealt with each situation like a pro.

They'd sat too long in the car and the last thing Cody wanted now was to sit in a chair and just listen. It irked him he couldn't see what was going on and he didn't want to appear as if he were hiding out any- more. So they stood by the wall.

"Hey, Cody." The voice was familiar, but it took Cody a second to put a face to the voice.

"It's been a long time."

He extended his hand and immediately felt the firm grasp of an old friend. "Yes, it has. How's it going, Stokes?" He quickly introduced him to Lyssa.

"I've been training Mystic Gypsy Queen these last months. I called the ranch a few times, but they said you weren't available."

That familiar burning ate away at Cody's gut, but he tamped down what he could and ignored the rest.

"I haven't been training these last few months."

As anxiety built inside him, Lyssa slipped her hand into his as if it was meant to be there. It felt good and he gave it a squeeze of thanks.

"That's what I heard. Heard you had some surgery, too, but that didn't work out. That's too bad."

Wonderful how good news gets around.

"You've got yourself a fine dog here."

"His name is Otis," Lyssa offered cheerfully.

Otis was sitting contently by his left leg. Cody didn't want to talk about the dog or his surgery or his failures, so he talked about something he knew would take attention away from him.

"It's good to see Gypsy competing. She's a fine horse."

"We've been out a few times, but my scores are shot."

"Who've you been training with?"

"That's just it, I haven't. Not since I was out at the Silverado. It's just been me and Gypsy."

"You were coming along just fine then."

"And I've been putting in time when I can, but I'm missing something and my scores have been disappointing."

"You might be doing too much on your own. Who do you have helping you choose your cattle?"

Stokes' laugh was hard. "No one but me. Do you know someone who can help me out?"

Cody thought for only a second. "You go talk to Wes Devlin. I've known him a long time and he's good at what he does. He can set you right and get you ready. In the meantime, you need to relax."

"I am relaxed."

Cody chuckled. "You're about as jumpy as a stray mouse caught in a rattlesnake den. If you're ready to jump out of your skin, you know Gypsy's going to sense it. It's going to put her on edge. When you're out there, stay in control."

"That may be why me and Gypsy seem to be one step behind the cow at every turn."

"Sounds like you may be getting in your horse's way. If you're leaning the wrong way into the turn she has to compensate for you and that's going to slow her down. Stay out of her way and let her do what she does best."

Stokes made a grunt that Cody took as understanding.

"And concentrate on what's coming up. Most of the riders up next aren't out here socializing with me or anyone else. They're watching the cows, getting their heads centered. The same goes for you. You need to watch the cattle and think about having a good run."

"I'd love to stop out at the ranch some time. Maybe get a few more pointers."

A vein in his neck jumped. Cody could feel his blood pounding hard, about to explode.

"I'm not sure how much help I'd be."

Stokes laughed hard. "You already have been."

"Good luck with your run, Stokes."

"It was good seeing you, Cody."

"You too," Cody said.

It was only an expression, one that didn't mean anything at all really, but Cody still swallowed the pain of the words.

Stokes said his goodbye to Lyssa just as the announcer came over the loudspeaker. The first rider for this set was getting his horse ready.

Lyssa asked some questions during the show and Cody answered them readily, but none of that was really what was on Cody's mind. He knew what his brother had done in bringing him here today. Beau hadn't needed him here to do much of anything. He was just here. Just off the ranch and among people. Despite knowing what his brother was up to, Cody found himself having a good time. He didn't know whether to be ticked off at Beau or to thank him.

But with every groan of the cattle, every hard stop of the horses sending dust flying every which way, Cody didn't want to be standing there watching. He wanted to be out there riding, on his horse, being a part of what he loved.

He could feel the rush crawling under his skin, reined in by the knowledge that he couldn't have it.

But oh, how he wanted it. He didn't think that yearning was ever going to go away.

The only thing this outing managed to do was multiply a craving for what Cody had hungered for his whole life.

Midnight was creeping around the corner when they'd made it back to Steerage Rock. Once again the house was quiet. Cody settled Otis into his room and came back downstairs to find Lyssa in the kitchen. It wasn't just that he'd heard the sound of running water. He could smell her subtle scent, feel her eyes on him, even though he couldn't see her.

Today he'd felt her beside him, grounding him even when nothing seemed steady. He liked that feeling a whole lot.

"You're good," she said, her voice blending in smoothly with the sound of the quiet evening.

"I thought you'd gone to bed. You must be tired after that long drive."

"I am, but I wanted to talk."

His lips tugged into a grin and he wagged his eyebrows. "About how good I am?"

She giggled and something inside him slipped free. "Something like that."

"I like the sound of that. Let's stop talking so I can show you just how good I am."

"I saw the way Stokes was looking at you. Like he was in awe. You have something to give. You're good at what you do."

"You got all that from watching Stokes?"

"Beau says you're one of the best."

A soft groan escaped his lips. "Beau says, huh? What about what I say? Doesn't that count for something?"

"It counts for everything."

"Good. Then I say you ought to be standing right here so I can hold you."

"You're not making this easy for me. At least Beau hasn't been acting like a fool."

"He has his moments."

"Not lately, as far as I've seen. What's with you

two anyway? Half the time you're at each other's throats, the other half . . ."

"You can say it. I'm not going to bark at you."

"It'd be a first."

She didn't offer any more than what she'd already revealed. She and Beau had shared some secrets in the arena that day when he'd stomped off. If he hadn't done an about-face, Cody would never have known.

"It's just our way, is all," he said quietly. "The way it's always been with all of us."

What else could he say? Lyssa didn't want to hear about old resentments, founded or otherwise, that had formed the bricks and mortar to built a wall between him and Beau.

Cody was acutely aware of Lyssa. He seemed to always be aware of every little move she made. And he liked that, too.

She was waiting.

"You're good," she repeated.

And then she waited again. For what, Cody wasn't quite sure. Maybe to challenge her by denying it. Maybe for him to push off a little arrogant attitude and admit it. He was good with cutting horses, good at training and riding.

At one time.

That hadn't been part of his life in a long time.

"You need eyes to do what I do. *Did.* I've said that before."

Her scent drew nearer and collided with his senses. He didn't want to reach out for her and find her not there. The thought of that left him cold. Lyssa not there. So he kept his hands cemented to his side. He could feel her, her subtle perfume mixing with the night air wrapping around him. She was close, but not close enough.

"You didn't need eyes today, Cody. Stokes just mentioned a few things he was doing and needing help with and you knew exactly what he was talking about. I didn't have a clue what those things meant, but you did."

"It's basic stuff."

"Maybe to you."

"To anyone who knows cutting. It wasn't a big deal. Any other trainer there today would have told him the same thing."

It irked Cody that maybe Stokes had come up to him out of pity. He sighed, his shoulders feeling the weight of too much thought. He finally decided that wasn't the case. Stokes was a good man who wouldn't waste his breath on pity for pity's sake.

"Stokes hasn't been around cutting all that long. Just had to be reminded about some things he already knew."

"What about someone new?"

Frustration grew inside him. He hated this distance.

"What about them?" Inching forward with his hands in front of him as a guide, he found the smooth counter and used it to move himself toward the sound of Lyssa's voice.

"Take me, for instance."

His face split into a wide grin when his fingers brushed against hers. Hooking his arms around her waist, he dragged her close to him. She leaned into him and his whole body drained of the tension he'd been feeling.

"I'm listening. I like that thought."

Lyssa giggled again. He was drawn to the quiet reserve of it, the slight intake of breath and the escape of laughter when she wasn't so self-conscious. He wanted to kiss her, to just bend his head and touch his lips to hers.

"You could train me."

Cody's arms went rigid. "You're kidding."

"No. I'm not. I thought it looked fun."

"Why?"

"Why was it fun?"

"Why do you want me to train you? What do you want to do this for?"

"I just . . . want to. That's all. Do I have to have a reason other than just wanting to try?"

"Is this a challenge?"

"No."

Sure it was, Cody thought, a bitter slice of pain leaving him raw right where he stood. Even if she didn't put it to words, he knew Lyssa was saying, "Cody, I challenge you to take a novice rider like me and teach her to ride a cuttin' horse. I challenge you to prove to me you don't need your eyes." She was almost begging him to stay the heck out of that chair by the pool and keep moving forward with life.

Reaching up, he scratched his jaw. "What about the training with Otis?"

"You're coming along. Both of you. There's plenty of time to do both. I don't have to leave for a while yet."

He laughed then. "You want me to train you in a few days."

"I still have a few weeks. I'd just like one or two lessons."

"Don't play with me, Lyssa," he growled. Abruptly, he released her and took a step back, away from the counter, away from Lyssa. *Into oblivion.* Retreating wasn't as easy as it used to be. He liked it a whole lot better when he had Lyssa in his arms, grounding him.

"What makes you think I am?"

He ignored the subtle hurt in her voice. "This isn't a challenge?"

"For me, yes."

She closed the distance he'd left when he stepped back, and slipped her arms around his waist, grounding him once again.

"I seem to recall you giving me some pretty strong words to the effect of me not really living. Not feeling that rush of life. I've . . . been thinking lately that maybe you're right."

Her voice was low and soft as a whisper.

"I want to feel that rush you talked about. I don't want to be afraid of feeling that."

"Darlin', holding you like this is enough to give any man a rush strong enough to cause a heart attack."

She laughed and seemed to melt into him. His head began to swim. "The things you say."

"I'll keep talking if it'll keep you here just like this. But truth be told, I'd rather be kissing you."

Lyssa reached up and cupped his cheeks with her hands, forcing him to bend his head. He felt the calluses there. She was a woman used to hard work. He admired her drive working with her dogs. Right now, he just loved the feel of her hands on his face and the light touch of her lips against his mouth.

"So what do you say?"

What had they been talking about? This woman had his head spinning like a lasso so much he couldn't keep a simple conversation straight.

"Training," he said with a slight grunt as he recalled the direction they'd been taking before Lyssa had distracted him.

"Yeah, will you do it?"

"What about training dogs?"

He felt her shrug. "You said yourself that there are plenty of weekend haulers out there who run businesses and work forty-hour-a-week jobs."

"Yeah, those same people train in the wee hours of the morning sometimes just to get some time in the saddle and then haul their horses around on the weekend competing. Those people may not get anywhere, or maybe they will. But most of the time it doesn't matter because they're doing what they love. And if you're not doing it because of that, because you love cuttin', then what are you doing it for?"

He hadn't intended his voice to sound so harsh. In truth, he just figured it was easier to let her know right from the get-go that he wasn't going to be played with. He wasn't her charity case. It was one thing to be dragged to a show and give a few words of encouragement to an old friend like Stokes. It was something entirely different to commit to training someone who had absolutely no knowledge or love of the sport.

Cody loved cutting. It had been his life. He hated the idea that maybe she was toying with him.

If there was one thing he knew Lyssa had caught on to was that he loved his horses and he loved cutting. It seemed odd that she would play with him this way. And he realized in that moment just how much he'd missed training.

Part of him wanted to believe that Lyssa wanted to do this for herself. Sharing that kind of excitement with her was something he could do in the privacy of his own ranch. It was a good reason to get up each day, if only to share that much with her.

Her chest pressed against his as she drew in her breath and then she sighed. "I'm not playing with you, Cody. I just want to give it a try."

When he didn't readily answer, she sighed again. It was a soft sound, a slight whisper of breath. He found himself wondering what it would feel like against his bare skin, his face, his lips. Good God, he wanted to end all this talk so he could kiss her again.

"Look, I don't know if I'm going to love cutting as much as you do or be any good at all. I really don't. But I think it might be kind of fun. And I want you to be the one to train me."

"What about after you leave?"

Cody didn't really want to think about Lyssa leaving, much less talk about it. But it always seemed to be there, niggling at the back of his mind.

Lyssa hesitated and he had to wonder why. "I really don't want to think about that right now." Her arms tightened around his waist. "Right now I just want to enjoy being right here in your world."

"Okay, I'll do it."

Something about Lyssa's words gave him pause. He liked having Lyssa around. He liked it even better when he had her wrapped in his arms like she was right at that moment.

And yeah, in his arms for the rest of his life sounded real good. He liked Lyssa being in his world, too. But it also terrified him. He didn't want pity. He desperately wanted what they shared right at that moment to be real.

Chapter Nine

They should have started earlier in the day when the sun wasn't so high and mightily cruel. The evenings teased with a cool chill that tended to make you believe spring was going to stick around just a little while longer. The days, however, were getting longer and hotter. The image of baking in the sun with her legs straddling an overworked animal wasn't too attractive to Lyssa.

But they weren't working outside. They were using the covered arena, which was cooler and more inviting. But if they had worked outside, it would at least hide the sudden attack of nerves that had her pooling with sweat.

They'd spent the morning in town with Otis. It seemed as though Otis and Cody had reached a level of comfort where Cody didn't need direction from Lyssa at all. She was just there. Just in case. *Invisible again.*

Something about that nagged at her like an insect bite. Sure, she was used to being invisible. But she found that she liked it a whole lot better when Cody knew she was with him. She felt like a part of him.

She liked being in his world.

Part of her knew it had been a bad idea to come to the ranch, even for all the good it did. The speed in which they'd managed to get through training was in part due to the enormous amount of one-on-one attention she'd been able to give Cody once he finally embraced the idea of working with Otis. He put his whole self into it and got back what he gave. For both of them.

She knew her dogs. She knew Otis was a special dog and that a kindred spirit moved inside both him and Cody. He had a sense of pride about him that Cody recognized. It was what made them the perfect match.

Pretty soon, a matter of days even, Cody wouldn't need direction from Lyssa at all. The two of them would manage as a team all on their own and they'd be fine. Without her.

Tamping down a pang of jealousy, Lyssa decided she was being ridiculous. She was beginning to think her life had turned into a sappy novel of sorts. Tears were common whenever she parted ways with one of her dogs. But the pride she felt, as well as the knowledge in knowing what the new handler and guide dog could accomplish together, always made up for any feelings of sorrow. Goodbyes were inevitable in every case. But the tears she shed were always happy ones.

That morning she'd woken wanting to burst into tears, but for entirely different reasons. Ones that were better off not explored. It was a lot harder to enjoy the time she had left knowing that the day she'd leave was growing closer with every sunrise.

She squinted as she stepped inside the door of the arena, pulling off her sunglasses to let her eyes adjust to the change of light. She stared into the arena, at the cattle Beau and Dirk had brought in, and she wanted to cry again.

What on earth had she been thinking when she'd asked Cody to train her? Had she lost her mind completely?

Well, that much was true enough. Every time Cody held her she was sure she'd lost her mind.

It had been a spur of the moment decision, an automatic reaction to his prodding about her not living her life. But on second thought . . .

No, she wouldn't cave. Feel the rush? Yeah, she wanted that again. That same sense of excitement she felt flying through the field that day when she'd all but forgotten her initial fear of riding. A fear that was replaced with the chilling thought of Cody about to become decapitated by a low-hanging branch if Sassy tore into those trees. For those few seconds, it had been exciting, nothing like anything she'd felt before.

But did she really have to prove herself by huddling among the cattle?

Cody was a man who had a lot to offer. He was good at what he did. She was in good hands. Cody's hands. And that was enough to ease her nerves somewhat.

"You have no choice," she told herself. "Your word isn't any good if you don't keep it."

"You feeling okay?" Beau asked as he came up alongside her on their way to where Cody and Dirk were standing. Otis, ever faithful, was sitting quietly by Cody's side.

"Sure, why wouldn't I be?"

"You're white as a sheet. Talking to yourself, too." Beau stopped walking as if to force her to stop and give him a second. He stared at her for a moment and said, "He's good, you know."

"I know that."

"What is it, then?"

"Nothing. I'm ready."

She said it as much for herself as for Beau. The last thing she wanted was for Cody to get wind that she was scared spitless.

She started toward Cody again and Beau followed alongside her.

"He won't say it, but he's as nervous about this as you are."

"I doubt that," Lyssa said under her breath. But apparently not quietly enough. Cody lifted his head in her direction. He'd either heard her mumbling or the sound of her boots. She wasn't sure which.

"You ready?" he asked. His face was a little skeptical, he chewed on his bottom lip for a moment and then stopped as if catching himself.

Her heart jumped all the same. *She could do this.* She was in good hands. Cody's hands.

"As ready as I'll ever be."

"You're not convincing me," he said with a quirk of a smile.

"Is that a requirement?"

His smile stretched out wide then, seeming to transform his whole face. "Lys, you've got nothing to prove."

Maybe not to you, she thought. Sighing, she felt her

chest constrict even though she was forcing out the air. If one thing had become clear in the last few days, it was that she had a whole lot to prove to herself. She couldn't walk around being afraid of her own shadow anymore.

"It's just . . . last night it all seemed like such a great idea. Watching the others ride got me thinking."

"And now?"

"Now, I don't know."

Her answer was as honest as she could be. She didn't want to back down from this.

"Cody, I've only just begun riding, for cripes sake. What the heck was I thinking? And now you're going to put me in the middle of all those cows as if I have a clue of what to do with them."

Her voice rose as hysteria bubbled up her throat. She drew in a deep breath of air in an effort to calm herself.

Cody chuckled softly, a sexy smile stretching his lips. "Lys, they're just cows. So what? You've only been riding a few times. Big deal." He adjusted his hat. "That just means you haven't had a chance to develop any bad habits I've got to help you break."

It wasn't at all what she'd expected him to say. "Really?"

"Yeah, I've trained lots of people who've had as much time in the saddle as you've had. It's not a problem at all."

He turned away from her and she heard his slow sigh. When he turned back, he sliced the air with his hand and said, "If you want to call this off—"

"No way," she blurted out quickly. She chewed her bottom lip. "Honestly, you think I can do this?"

"It doesn't much matter what I think, Lyssa."

"Yes, it does. It matters to me."

"Why are you doing this?"

His question shouldn't have thrown her off guard, but somehow it did. With a quick motion, she wiped her sweaty palms down the sides of her jeans.

"Because I want to."

"You said that. But why? It's obvious you're not standing there itching to get into that saddle. So what's making you?"

"You."

His shoulders sagged slightly and the rest of his body went rigid. It was clearly not the answer he was looking for. But it was honest.

"I told you last night. You said I wasn't living," she said by way of explanation.

He lifted his head. "That's really why you're doing this?"

"Yes."

She looked away and put her arm lengthwise along the rail, resting her head against it. He couldn't see her, she knew that. But she kept her face averted anyway.

"It's because I realized you were right. About everything. I don't like it very much, but I know what you were trying to tell me. I hide out. I use my dogs as a way to keep myself busy so I don't have to explore anything new. Anything about life that might . . . hurt me. I'm not much of a risk-taker."

She watched his face, waiting for his reaction, and wondered if he knew how much the truth of what she admitted had to do with her feelings for him. When Cody made no response, she added, "All those things I'm afraid of."

He nodded his understanding and a smile crept into his cheeks. *Lord, he was so handsome when he smiled.* It only fueled all those fears that had her pulling away from him that night when they'd danced and he'd first kissed her.

"It's okay to be nervous."

She wondered whether he was talking about getting back on the horse or about him. Being with Cody, it didn't matter where or how, it was as if she couldn't breathe.

Focus.

"Okay, let's do it."

"Riding a cuttin' horse is a lot like dancing. You and the horse are partners, you blend, become one. When it happens right it's real pretty to watch. Just like dancing."

Her cheeks flamed, thinking about that night when they'd gone to the club to see Brock sing. "You've already experienced my dancing."

He chuckled. "You're thinking too much again, Lys. You have to rely on feeling. But for now we're just going to talk a bit, get you used to what's going on, get you comfortable in the saddle."

A smile tugged at her lips. "And then we dance."

He smiled right back at her and she had to catch her breath.

"That's right."

Cody whistled, just as he had when they'd been out riding that first time and he'd called to Sassy. This time, Otis perked up and came alongside him. Cody bent down and gave him a word of praise, scratching behind Otis' ears before picking up the leash and giving him the command to move forward.

Lyssa stood a second, stuck in her tracks with a mixture of amazement and delight. When had that happened? When had the two of them connected so completely that Otis was now responding to a command she hadn't even taught him?

She moved behind them, confidence building inside her with each step.

One of the hands was bringing in a horse, already saddled and ready.

"I just assumed since Diesel E is the horse I've been riding that I'd be riding him today."

"We'd put you on Diesel because he's a good horse for a beginning rider. He's predictable and sound."

"Predictable. That sounds good to me. I like predictable."

"He's not a cuttin' horse though."

"There's a difference?"

"A big difference. This is Whole Lotta Magic. She's a pretty paint quarter horse. Most cutting horses are quarter horses, although there are other breeds that are trained to compete. She's an experienced horse. She was the first horse I worked with when I started training on my own and she did real well in competition. She knows what she's doing and won't rely heavily on you for direction. That's what you need now. It'll give you the chance to get comfortable in the saddle and get used to the moves."

"Okay. That just went way over my head."

"Don't worry. We'll take it slow."

"Maybe I should just watch Beau for a bit."

"No chickening out."

With a little help from Beau, she mounted Magic and moved in the saddle until it felt right.

"How does it feel?"

"Like I'm sitting in a saddle."

Cody tossed her a wry grin. "Don't be difficult. Think of yourself sitting in your favorite chair."

"Just as long as we're not talking about that chair by the pool."

Cody pulled his hat off and dragged his hand over his head. When he lifted his head again to reposition his hat she saw he was smiling.

"Fair enough," he said. "Now relax. I can tell you're about to jump right out of your skin."

Relax. That was easy for him to say. His boots were still firmly on the ground.

"You've got two riders who are going to keep the cattle centered in the pen. Just let things happen, don't try to make them happen."

Lyssa breathed in deeply and watched the cattle moving around, heard their groaning pleas to be left undisturbed, and was lost to what Cody was saying.

"You with me?" he asked.

"Yeah."

Still, she clung white-knuckled to the saddle horn as Cody took the reins and with Otis, led her into the arena. Cody gave commands to Otis like he was as used to working with a guide dog as with a horse. All the while he explained the basics of what Lyssa had to do.

"Everyone is as nervous as you before their run. Cuttin' is both physically and mentally draining, so you need to stay focused on what you want to accomplish. And that's to have a good time."

She peered down at Cody when he stopped at the opening to the arena.

"Okay."

As nervous as she was, excitement nevertheless roared through her.

"You still with me, Lys?"

"Comfy chair. I'm there," she said, giving him a thumbs-up she knew he couldn't see.

He chuckled. "Good girl."

Beau had already mounted his horse and was working with Dirk to contain the herd of cattle on the far side of the working area.

"I'm all set, Cody," he called out. "The rest of the riders are in place."

Cody explained the process of approaching the herd slowly, so as not to disturb the cattle. How to separate one cow from the herd and signal the horse.

"Once you've indicated to your horse which cow you want to cut, you need to loosen the reins, then your horse takes over. This is where the real action is, where a good cutting horse can show good cow sense. She'll be lightning quick, going head to head with the cow to keep her from returning to the herd."

"And what am I supposed to do while Magic's doing all that?" Lyssa asked, her head reeling.

"Think about your feet, darlin', and enjoy the ride."

They talked a bit more and as she listened, Lyssa wondered how on earth she was going to be able to remember all the things she needed to remember and still manage to stay in the saddle with all those quick stops and turns she'd seen the horses make at the competition. She'd be lucky if she didn't land facedown in the dirt.

Cody seemed to sense her anxiety and a quick word or two, coupled with that high-voltage smile of his, put her at ease. Throughout, the sound of his voice, the rich tone that held an air of authority and reassurance, penetrated her and remained. It was enough to allay her anxiety, at least for the moment.

Then it was her turn to ride with Magic into the herd. Beau had pointed out a few cows that were slower and wouldn't be too hard for a first run. From the sidelines, Cody remained quiet, unable to see where she was or what she was doing. Still, she felt him there with her, heard his voice in her head, urging her on. His confidence in her made all the difference in the world.

"When you've moved your chosen cow out far enough away from the main herd, loosen the reins to give Magic some leeway to move," Cody called out from the sidelines.

And when Lyssa did, it all happened so fast. With a shock of adrenaline Magic bounded forward, heading off the cow. Lyssa held tight to the saddle horn with one hand and tried to remember where her feet were supposed to be. Still she flew back and forth, barely able to hold herself secure with each lightning-quick stop and then immediate turn in the opposite direction.

Her pulse pounded in her head, her breath caught in her throat. She held tight to the saddle horn, her eyes glued to the distraught cow in front of her who wanted nothing more than to get out of this horse's way. As if admitting defeat, the cow just stopped and turned away. Lyssa pulled up on the reins, signaling to Magic that the run was over.

It was only then that Lyssa felt a stabbing pain in her mouth and realized she'd sunk her teeth into her lip. But she didn't care. Her heart was pounding with a charge like she'd never known.

She was vaguely aware of voices, Beau talking to Cody or Dirk or maybe both. She rode over to the railing and jumped out of the saddle.

Cody heard Lyssa's laughter over the voices and wished with all his heart and soul he could see her face. He wanted to see Lyssa's smile, see the spark of light dancing in her eyes that went with the triumphant laughter. It didn't matter how she did, or what mistakes she'd made, not that he could tell. He hadn't been able to see her ride. But she'd loved it. He could hear it in her laughter.

She flew against him, winding her arms around his neck, nearly knocking him back against the rail, still laughing.

"My God, Cody, it was amazing!" she said, her words coming out in a burst of breath.

His head was spinning and his insides seemed to jump to life. Lord, how he loved her laugh.

She kissed him and he tasted blood. His heart sank. "Lyssa, you cut yourself." He touched her lip and felt the wetness.

"It's nothing. I must have bit my lip."

He kissed her again lightly so as not to hurt her.

When she drew back her voice was quiet, but still held the same excitement he'd heard just moments ago. "I wish you could have seen me, Cody."

The lump he had to swallow was big and hard, but he managed it somehow. He would give anything to have been able to see her ride. But he felt it deep down. And she was sharing it with him even if he couldn't experience it himself. That rush. She felt it and now through her, he felt it too.

"I did see it, darlin'. I did."

She held onto him tightly, laughing. "When can I do it again?"

Chapter Ten

*O*h, *sweet, merciful Mother of God, who was the evil heathen who invented the saddle?* Lyssa thought as she peeled off her blue jeans that evening. Her thighs were screaming at her, never mind her backside. And they had every right to. She didn't want to look in the mirror and see what hidden part of her had turned shades of blue or purple. She could feel it. Seeing it would only lend a new degree of assault to her already battered body.

Steam rose from the spout as hot water flowed into the tub in her whirlpool bath. Lyssa hadn't thought she'd need such a luxury when she'd first arrived at the ranch, but now she knew without a doubt that it was an essential part of living here. She couldn't imagine how these cowboys could sit day in and day out astride a horse, using muscles she didn't even realize existed on her body until today, and not feel like they'd been run over by a truck.

The only place she was going to sit for a good long while was the bathtub. No wonder they all walked around bowlegged, for cripes sake. Nature had to take care of such things over time. But Lyssa wasn't about to wait for nature.

She climbed into the tub and turned on the jets. Immediately her aching muscles cried out in relief. Leaning her head back against the soft headrest, she smiled, thinking about the day. It had truly been incredible. For all her talk about Cody staying out of his chair by the pool, Lyssa realized she'd stayed in a chair of sorts for the last few years herself. Cody had opened her eyes to that and had given her a gift like nothing else she'd experienced.

He'd made her feel invincible. His confidence in her and his gentle words of encouragement managed to overshadow what confidence she lacked. She had come out the better for it.

She had realized almost immediately that she truly wanted Cody to be able to see her ride. It wasn't his fault. She just wanted to share that amazing feeling with him.

He said she had, that he had felt her excitement and that it made it all worthwhile.

To what end?

She dunked her whole body under the foamy water, dousing her hair, and emerged again, pushing back the wet tendrils of hair that had fallen in her face.

There was something special about that man to cause her heart to race like it did. *Feel that rush.* How long it was likely to last, she had no idea. The way Cody smiled at her, held her in his embrace, made the world tilt on its axis. She didn't want it to end.

But it would. She was going to be on the ranch only another week or two. So many things would change. Cody expected to have another operation soon and she would go back to Houston to continue training her dogs.

Something prickly nagged at the nape of her neck. She felt the urge to reach back and brush it away, but she knew it wouldn't help. What nagged at her wasn't something visible. It was the fear that one day Cody *would* open his eyes and see her. Really see her. And all the wonderful feelings he evoked in her, all the things he thought he saw, would just be an illusion.

And the rush would end for both of them.

It was common, she knew. She'd been on both ends. First as a student, looking up to Chad and all he seemed to be, both to her and for her. And then as a teacher herself. All too often, a student mistook feelings of gratitude for love. And after a time, those mistaken feelings became crystal clear.

It would probably end that way for her and Cody. Right now, he saw her as the one person who'd opened a door that had been cemented shut.

Lyssa's heart sank and she had to swallow to keep her body from trembling. She couldn't change fate, but she could enjoy the gifts that life offered her today. For now that would have to be enough.

They sat under the same tree as they had that first day they'd gone riding. They sat in the same spot where he'd held her face in his hands.

Lyssa stifled a sigh. The very last thing she wanted to be was nostalgic or sentimental. But there was some degree of that floating around in her subconscious. Something she'd only really begun to see.

There would soon come a day when she'd leave the Silverado Ranch. She couldn't help but wonder what she'd bring away with her as a keepsake of her time here. No, nothing practical or even tangible. It was more. Something that only Cody was able to see.

"What's so funny?" he asked, opening up the picnic basket Isadore had helped her prepare that morning.

She hadn't realized she had laughed aloud at the irony, but apparently she had.

"Nothing."

Unconvinced, he gave her a wry grin. "You're a better liar than that."

"I was just wondering how you knew. That's all."

"About the right thing to have for lunch? It's all about hunger, Lyssa."

She rolled her eyes. "I wasn't talking about food."

Bending over, she lifted the blue cloth napkins and stoneware plates out of the picnic basket they'd brought along. Her hand brushed against the bottle of wine she was sure wasn't there when they'd finished packing the basket earlier and wondered if it had been Isadore or Cody who'd slipped it inside, along with two crystal wine glasses.

She didn't have to wonder long.

"We're celebrating," Cody said.

"Oh? What's the occasion?"

He poured the wine into two glasses he held by the stems between two fingers, a half grin tilting his mouth.

"I can think of many things to celebrate. Your riding for one thing. You've come a long way."

"Thanks to you."

"No, you're good. A natural, even."

"How do you know for sure? Maybe I've been fooling you all this time and had Beau sitting on that horse for me."

He shrugged and handed her one of the glasses.

"I'd know."

"Yeah, I know you would."

"Your laughter is proof enough how much you love it. That's not likely to change. It won't be long before you're competing."

"It's kind of like a fever, isn't it? Once you catch it, you have it."

"I know a thing or two about fevers lately."

Something told her there was more that Cody wasn't saying. "So you brought me out here to celebrate how well I'm doing? Or was there something else?"

"I got the call from my doctor this morning. My eyes are healed enough to have the corneal replacement surgery. I'm going in next week. Only one eye this time, but that's enough. A new technique they're going to try out on me increases the chances of this graft taking. It's still a long shot, and there's no guarantee the new cornea won't be rejected. But if all goes well, I'll be looking into your blue eyes by next week. And that, darlin', is definitely something to celebrate."

He raised his glass in the air a little and she met him halfway with her own without even thinking. Even as the clink of crystal meeting crystal sounded in the distant hum of animals and insects, a cold dread built up in the pit of her stomach. Lyssa immediately fought to squash it down.

Tears sprang to her eyes. She was being ridiculous. This was truly a wonderful thing for Cody. Sure, the chances that his surgery would take were still iffy. But there was always hope. Sometimes all you had was hope. And she knew firsthand that technology was changing every day. For Cody's doctor to want to try again, he had to feel some confidence that this time it would work. Surely he'd spare Cody the heartbreak otherwise.

"That's wonderful, Cody. You must be thrilled."

"If it's so wonderful, how come you're not giving me a big hug?"

Lyssa closed her eyes and sighed. He was way too good at reading her. His smile faltered as he said the words. She wanted so much to be in his arms right then. But she feared he'd see right through her. And she didn't quite know how to put these irrational feelings she'd been having into words.

Still, it wasn't fair to deny him the joy he felt. Putting the wine glass down, she leaned closer to him. She pushed off his hat, and taking his face in her hands, she kissed him. It was sweet and quick and she had to suck in a breath for fear a sob would escape her lips.

He smiled, reaching his arm around her to give her a squeeze. "That's better. Now I have a favor to ask."

"What's that?"

"I'd like you to be there for the surgery."

"While you're having it?"

He shook his head. "Not in the room. I'd just like it if you were there. I know it'll probably be boring hanging around during the operation. It's just . . ."

She closed her eyes. "Cody, I'm not sure I'm even going to be here next week."

There, she'd said it. They'd both put off talking about her leaving.

Cody didn't immediately react to the news. He just sat there, lifted his glass to his lips, and took another sip of wine as if weighing her words as he would savor the first drop of wine.

He cleared his throat. "What's so pressing that you need to go running off now?"

"Nothing that hasn't been there all along. My work."

He simply nodded.

"The school was prepared for me to be here the four weeks, but now . . ."

"You've finished your business here?"

Her shoulders sagged and she pulled away from him, glancing down at her hands folded in her lap.

"Cody, you don't need me anymore. You really haven't needed me for days now. But other students do."

"I see. I thought you liked being here at the ranch."

Her heart broke, and she had to clamp her teeth down on her bottom lip to keep it from quivering. "I do."

His lips lifted a fraction. "Then there's no reason you can't stay for a while longer."

"There's another class starting in a matter of days. Other students that need to be trained. It's time for me to go home."

Even as she said the words they gnawed at her.

"Other students, huh?"

"It was never supposed to be forever, Cody."

She said the last part quietly, almost to herself, as if it would somehow convince her too.

"Things are different now than when you came here."

Her heart ached just thinking about it. Things had changed, for her anyway. She'd fallen in love with Cody, despite knowing it would only hurt her in the end.

She pushed an errant strand of hair from her face

that the wind insisted on forcing back in front of her eyes. "In some ways nothing has changed."

He laughed. "Darlin', a whole lot has changed for me since the day you stepped onto that patio by the pool. You mean to tell me I'm wrong about that? I wasn't just dreaming about you being in my arms, Lys. You were there. Both of us together."

"My reason for being here hasn't changed."

"Why should it change anything?"

"Because it does. I have to leave, Cody." *Or I'm never going to know if what you feel for me is real.* "I'm your instructor. You're my student. Feelings have a way of getting mixed up in a situation like ours."

"Funny. All this time I was thinking . . ."

"What?"

"That what we had was special. A relationship."

She smiled, but didn't feel it in her heart. "Of course it is, Cody. We've become close."

His voice dripped with sarcasm as he spoke. "Close. Is that how you see us?"

Lyssa fought the tears that were filling her eyes, but one escaped anyway and slowly trailed down her cheek. "I like being with you, Cody."

He simply nodded.

"You don't understand," she said, shaking her head.

"No, I hear what you're saying, Lyssa. There's never been anything wrong with my hearing."

She inched closer to him, wanting to reach her hand up to touch him, but held herself back. "No, I don't think you really do. You see, I've been here before. I know what it's like to have someone come into your world and change it. I'd been with Chad for over a year and I thought I loved him."

Cody turned away from her, effectively shutting her

out as far as she could tell. But she reached for him, placing her hands on both sides of his face, forcing him to face her, even if he couldn't see her. She needed him to understand.

"Chad was my instructor and I thought he was my world. What I didn't know until I was finally able to see with my eyes was that he was in love with my sister."

Cody mumbled something under his breath that Lyssa was sure she didn't need to know.

"Thing is, as crushed as I was at first, I realized that I wasn't actually seeing Chad for who he was. There were a lot of things I had refused to see about us because I really wanted what I thought we had to be real."

"And it wasn't?"

"No. I thought I needed him. I thought he was my soul mate, if you believe in such things. And I did. But I realized soon after we broke up that I'd made up a lot of what I thought we had because I wanted it to be true. And everything we didn't have had been plain the whole time. I just didn't want to see it."

"You think I'm doing that with us."

She closed her eyes. "I don't know. I really don't. All I know is that when I leave here, you're going to be fine without me."

"No, I need you, Lys." He reached for her hand, stroking her skin with his fingers.

"You think you do. But you're going to be fine without me, Cody."

The tears she fought to hold back fell freely now. "This wasn't one-sided, Cody. Being here with you has made me find something I didn't know existed in me before."

He wrapped his arms around her and pulled her to him. "Then what are you so afraid of now? That my feelings for you aren't real? Because let me tell you, there's never been anything that has felt more real to me in my life that this, holding you like this. Or is this something you're not willing to take a risk on?"

"I've never been much for risks."

"I thought it could be . . . never mind. Drink your wine."

She stared down at the glass she'd propped on the blanket before she'd moved closer to Cody. It was too far to reach.

No matter. Lyssa didn't much feel like celebrating. But this wasn't about them. It never really was. A few kisses. Some softly spoken words didn't make reality any different. It didn't mean they were forever.

Truth was, Lyssa truly did want it to be forever. But some crucial things hadn't even come into play yet. Cody needed to think about his surgery. And Lyssa wanted so desperately for him to see her exactly as he saw her now. She wanted him to always believe she was the beautiful woman he saw in his mind. And she desperately wanted to believe that all these feelings he felt for her were real. If he got his eyesight back, he wouldn't need her reassuring hand anymore. He wouldn't look at her the same way at all.

"I need to check in with Catherine, the director of the school. If it means that much to you that I be there for your surgery, then I'll be there." They had, at the very least, a friendship that she wouldn't deny or ignore. And she would be there for Cody even if the next few days were nothing but torture.

"It does," he said, his voice very quiet. "Thank you."

No matter how strong a man Cody was, he was still afraid and Lyssa recognized the fear his voice held. Her heart ached for him as she recalled the fright she'd felt just before her operation. There was always hope for a miracle, but it was riddled with a gnawing fear that that miracle would never come.

Cody had already undergone surgery before, only to be denied his miracle. Something told Lyssa that this time around they were both going to need one.

The morning of Cody's surgery had come quicker than anyone had anticipated. It brought with it both anticipation and anxiety for Lyssa. Cody could possibly be able to see the world around him again. But that meant Lyssa had to leave.

Beau was already in the kitchen when she walked in that morning. Cody was still upstairs, tending to Otis and packing an overnight bag for his stay at the hospital. Beau poured himself a cup of coffee and joined her at the table before he said a word.

"Isadore asked me to give this to you before she left for the market," he said, sliding a folded pink slip of paper across the table.

Lyssa swallowed a sip of coffee before reaching for the slip and giving it a quick glance. She groaned when she read the message from Catherine. She folded the paper and stuffed it in her pocket.

Beau stared down into his cup. "He's not the same man he was when you first got here."

"No, he's not."

"Never thought I'd see it. He's actually smiling. Half the time I don't even think he knows it, but you've gone and made him happy. It's the darnedest thing."

"It's not me, it's him."

Beau looked at her directly. "You underestimate yourself and what you do for him."

Lyssa shook her head and laughed. "You're giving me too much credit, and you underestimate him. You've all been doing it for months. When a person gets down like Cody was, it's hard to see a way out. But now he's done it. He's climbed out of that hole. No matter what happens with this surgery, I don't think he'll be going back."

"That was one heck of a climb."

"Yes, it was."

"I'm glad you were there to help him."

"I didn't do anything more than my job, Beau."

"Didn't you?"

"I did my job. Cody did the rest."

Beau sighed, leaning back in his chair. "I haven't been around much these last few years, but I know my brother. He's not one to come right out and say what's on his mind unless he's ticked off. And then he says plenty. Unfortunately, I've been on the receiving end of that on more occasions than I care to mention."

A smile tugged at her lips. "He says what needs to be said."

"I hope so. And if he's not, I hope you're looking at his words real hard and reading between the lines."

Leaning forward, Beau rested his elbows on the table, arms crossed in front of him. "There aren't a whole lot of women who would have lasted past that first afternoon with Cody, never mind a month. You're still here. And he's listening to you. You're like a beacon of light to him and I can see it. That says something to me."

Lyssa was quiet, weighing her thoughts before she spoke. She and Cody hadn't hidden their relationship from anyone over the past few weeks. They'd kissed passionately in front of a crowd of people at the dance hall. And there wasn't anyone on the ranch who hadn't witnessed some form of affection they'd expressed these last few weeks. But they didn't know reality as she knew it.

She stifled a sigh as she rose from the table and poured her coffee down the drain of the sink. She didn't want to delve into those issues now with Beau. She'd tossed them around in her head a hundred times over the past few nights, wondering if she was being fair to Cody and to herself. All she knew for sure was that this message from Catherine meant the clock had run out on any time that she and Cody had had.

"I'll be leaving the ranch and going back to Houston."

Lyssa didn't volunteer the fact that she should have already gone. She should have left a week ago. If Catherine had had her way, she'd already be back at the school.

But something kept her here at the ranch. Cody. Breaking away from what she felt for him in her heart was the hardest thing she'd ever had to deal with.

"I know," Beau said.

"I promised Cody I'd stay for his surgery. It's important to him that I be there. After all he's been through, I'm not going to let him down. But the deal was for me to stay only a month."

"You can wrap your feelings around any kind of deal you want if it makes you happy, Lyssa. I don't care. All I'm saying is that it's real nice having you here. And I like seeing my brother happy. Maybe you should think about working that into one of your deals."

She smiled and turned to face him, tears stinging her eyes. "Have you always played matchmaker for Cody?"

Beau chuckled and shook his head. "Heck no. He can do that pretty well on his own. I just want to make sure he's not fool enough to let the one good thing in his life slip through his hands."

She couldn't help it. A blush rose, thick and hot, from her toes to her eyebrows. Charm ran deep and strong in the Gentry men. She ought to know. She was well over the moon in love with one of them.

The procedure lasted no more than an hour. Cody had been through it before, pacing himself through every step with his nerves eating his insides. The cornea was to be placed in his left eye, the one that was less damaged—not that it had mattered the first time. The graft still hadn't taken.

"I'm getting ready to drop the new cornea in place, Cody," Dr. Curtis said. "Let me know what you see, if anything."

Immediately upon contact darkness became light and he could see. Cody wanted to blink, but his eyelids were pulled apart to prevent him from doing so. Nothing was clear. Dr. Curtis dripped a few drops in his eye to moisten it and within a few seconds the blurriness began to subside.

"Anything?" the doctor asked.

"Yes."

Cody's heart swelled and he wanted to break down and cry. The fear he felt inside was just too palpable. To have his sight, even for only a moment, seemed like a miracle. The chance of this graft not taking was the same as it had been before. His burns had been deep. But there was hope. Always hope.

His voice was slurred from the medication they'd given him. "Before you put the bandage over my eyes, I'd like for my friend to come in. Just for a second. I want to see her."

Friend. It sounded almost insignificant saying it that way. Lyssa was more than just a friend. Much more. But what were they? She was leaving. What did that say about them? Friends could leave. Cody would give anything to have her stay.

The doctor concentrated on suturing the eye, and spoke slowly as he concentrated. "I understand how anxious you are to test out this new vision, Cody. Believe me, I do. But I don't want to take any chance at all of introducing bacteria into this sterile environment and risking another rejection. You'll only have the bandage on for a few days. I promise you it will be worth the wait."

Cody squashed the deep sense of disappointment that engulfed him. Dr. Curtis couldn't know that a few days might be too late. But Cody wouldn't risk it if it meant never seeing again. It made him all the more determined to convince Lyssa that she had to stay. At least for another few days.

The little pink phone message Beau had handed Lyssa before they'd left for the hospital was burning a hole in her pocket. There was nothing to do in the waiting room but wait. Staring at the writing on the paper for the millionth time wasn't going to change the words.

She hadn't told Cody she'd stay beyond the surgery and now she had no choice.

Pulling out the paper for the umpteenth time in the last hour, she glanced at the neatly scripted message.

The baby came earlier than Sharon expected. By a whole month! And Jerry has already left on his vacation. I need you now!

If Catherine could have granted her a few more days, Lyssa knew she would have. They were in dire straits. Students for the new class were already on their way to Houston from all over the country. Classes would start in just two days. And Lyssa was totally unprepared.

It had been more than a month since she'd been with the dogs. She hadn't even had a chance to scan any of the applications to see who might be a good match. Catherine had gone through the list, but she said that she needed someone who knew the dogs, someone who knew the idiosyncrasies of each and could judge if the chosen person was the right match. Those first few days were so critical for new students, their hopes so high for success. The school needed to be fully staffed to ensure that success. With two people down, that left Lyssa to fill the gap.

And she was unprepared.

Lyssa knew she needed some time with the dogs. Just a day or two to refresh her memory. That meant leaving tonight, tomorrow at the latest, to get a full day in before the new class arrived.

"Oh, Cody," she whispered to herself in the waiting

room as she leaned her head back against the wall. A tear she'd fought mightily to hold back slipped down her cheek. She swiped it clean with a brush of her hand. "I hope you can forgive me."

Chapter Eleven

Cody woke with a start, feeling the bedrail just to be sure. Yes, he was in his own bed. He'd talked the doctor out of making him stay the night at the hospital after promising to go to his office first thing in the morning to check on his eyes. He'd left the hospital with Lyssa and a bag filled with bandages and eyedrops to wet his eye just in case it became too dry.

He lifted himself up in bed and dropped his feet to the floor with a thud. The pine planks were cool to his soles. He'd gotten use to his magnified senses, except for the fact that every morning the floor felt like a block of ice instead of cool wood beneath his feet.

Otis was awake and alert, Cody figured, from the rattle of his tags and the scrape of his paws against the floor. A wet nose nudged his arm, giving him further proof.

Lyssa was going to leave him. Cody couldn't think of anything more insane than that.

She had her reasons, she'd said. And he was sure they were valid. She was good at what she did and

168

Cody knew there were a lot more people she could help. But Cody could think of a thousand reasons why she shouldn't leave him to her one reason why she should.

"She doesn't think I need her anymore," he told Otis, who gave a loud yawn and sank back to the floor, his paws scraping against the polished surface.

"I mean, what kind of reason is that for leaving a man you . . ."

And it dawned on him. Yeah, he was in love with Lyssa. From her sunshine laugh to the soft feel of her silky hair to her spit-and-vinegar tongue. He had it bad for her. Maybe even since the day she first came and told him Otis was here to stay. Certainly since the day she stood at the pool flaming mad, dripping wet, and made him follow her with sodden clothes.

And she was leaving. *You don't need me anymore,* she'd said.

"Yeah, I do, Lyssa," Cody said quietly to himself. "Just not in the way you think."

In darkness, it was easier to bear. He couldn't see her face, her eyes. She couldn't see his eyes behind his sunglasses. She couldn't read all the emotions he didn't even understand that were coursing through him like a freight train running through the cold night. Deep in the darkness he'd lived in these past months, he'd gotten used to hiding.

He touched the bandage covering his eye and sighed, deep and long. In the light, he could fight. He could look into Lyssa's eyes and see the emotion she held for him, not just guess or hope that it was real. He could see it and he could feel it. That's what he wanted.

Patting Otis on the head, Cody rose to his feet. "Come on, boy. We've got some work to do."

He made his way to the bathroom, using his hands to guide him, letting Otis stay to the left side of him when he knew all he had to do was put on the leash and the dog would lead him where he needed to go without incident. He felt the smooth, cold porcelain of the sink and leaned his thigh against it, steadying himself. His hands trembled as he pulled the gauze from his eye, then the hard plastic cup that protected it from injury.

Blinking, Cody reeled from the light that filled his vision. It stung at first and then eased as he squinted against the assault of brightness. Then he blinked. Then again.

It wasn't just snatches of light that flashed in his mind. It was his face. Cody was staring at his reflection in the mirror for the first time in eight months. He brought his hand to his cheek and touched the light stubble on his chin, then turned to look at his hand, flexing it and wiggling his fingers. They seemed bigger, wider and harsher than he remembered. But they were his. Strong capable hands that held the ability to work and be useful again. That connection was one he hadn't had in a very long time.

Tears rose up inside him, emotion lodging in his throat. The surgery had worked. He had his miracle. He had his life back.

The distance from his eyes to the floor seemed more pronounced than Cody remembered. Vision in only the one eye had him a little off-balance. It had only been eight months, but in that time, he'd lost some of his bearings.

Cody needed to see Lyssa. Anticipation raced

through him. He wanted to see her, to look into her eyes while he heard her sweet voice talking to him. He wanted that connection like nothing he'd ever known.

With his hand braced on the wall of the hallway, he guided himself down to Lyssa's bedroom. Dr. Curtis had said it would take a while to reorient himself and gain his equilibrium. But it didn't matter. He still moved as fast as he could.

The door to her bedroom was ajar when Cody reached it. He knocked as he pushed it aside and stepped in, his heart about to explode out of his chest.

And then as quickly as it had risen, his heart plunged. Everything in Lyssa's room was neat and in place, as it had been the day she'd arrived at the Silverado Ranch. With the exception of Otis sitting by his leg, Cody didn't think there was a noticeable trace of evidence that Alyssandra Orchid McElhannon was ever here. *Except for the throbbing ache in his chest.*

He threw open the top drawer of the dresser just for further proof of what he already knew. It was empty, as was the closet.

As he turned to go back into the hallway, his good eye caught a glimpse of an envelope propped against a pillow on the bed. He would have laughed at the irony if didn't make him feel so dead inside. He could finally see. And he knew without a doubt he didn't want to see what was written in the letter Lyssa had left for him to read.

With a sigh, he moved his legs toward the bed with deliberate force and sank onto the firm mattress. Picking up the envelope, he turned it in his hands a few times and stared at it before tearing the seal.

Otis whined at his feet and slid down to the floor.

As Cody read the letter, he reached down to scratch Otis on the top of his head. Otis replied with a slap of his tail against the polished wood floor.

Dear Cody,

If you're reading this, then let me be the first to congratulate you on the success of your surgery. I'm so very thrilled for you. Truly, I am.

I knew you wouldn't wait for Dr. Curtis to take off your bandage. I think even he knew that.

Just so you know, I left early because I didn't see any reason for me to stay and prolong an already difficult parting. I didn't take Otis with me because he's your dog. You own him and you've become such a good team together. And if the surgery hadn't worked, I knew you wouldn't give up trying, but you'd need Otis to help you along. He's a gift and he would have given you much of your life back had you needed him to. But like the same engine that drives you, Otis needs a purpose. He's been trained to do a job and he needs to feel useful. Just like you. If you have your eyesight back, no matter how much you love him, he won't feel complete. He'll become depressed. I know you've gotten attached to him and he's a wonderful part of your life now, but I ask you to give both Otis and someone else the gifts he has to offer if you no longer need him. It's your decision.

You haven't needed my help in a long time. I should have left long before now, but for some reason I just couldn't. I don't want to wake up one morning and find out we were just an illu-

sion. I want to remember what we shared as being real. It was for me.

    Good luck, Cody. I'll be seeing you.
    Alyssandra

The paper crumpled easily in his hands under the weight of his frustration. She'd left without so much as saying goodbye. Nothing. Just *I'll be seeing you.*

What the heck was that supposed to mean? He hadn't really expected her to say something as stupid as *all my love* or *I'll love you always* just because he made the colossal mistake of falling in love with the woman.

Sighing, Cody rose from the bed, shoved the crumpled letter into the envelope, and tossed them into the wastepaper basket next to the nightstand. He nailed it on the first try. Funny how he felt no sense of triumph.

Sweet Sassy's Smile was dancing away in the arena. Beau was riding her, of course, and although Cody longed to be the one in the saddle, it didn't hurt quite as much as it had in past months. His time was coming soon.

Otis, who sat ever patiently by his side, had become his shadow even though now Cody didn't require him to wear his special leash. These past few weeks since Lyssa had gone, he'd been a comfort and a friend. Just like Lyssa had said.

"You've done a fine job with her, Beau," Cody called out when his brother finished the run.

Beau rode up along the rail, pulled off his hat, and shook the dust out of it with a quick slap against his chaps.

"I just finished the polish. Sassy got everything she needed from you, Cody."

"I appreciate that."

"You're itching to get into the saddle and try her out yourself. I can tell."

Cody laughed. "It's that obvious?"

"I've known you my whole life, Cody. There ain't a whole lot about you I don't know. You haven't gone and gotten patient on me, have you? I don't know if I can stand that."

"Afraid not. You're just going to have to put up with my bad moods."

"How long are you going to wait?"

"Doc Curtis said to be on the safe side I shouldn't do any kind of jarring activity for at least six to eight months. So I'll be on the sidelines at least until then."

"I was talking about Lyssa," Beau said, adjusting his straw hat on his head.

Cody nodded, feeling his gut squeeze the life out of him. "There aren't any guidelines to follow on that front."

"Lord, you can be such a hard-headed fool, Cody. Why don't you try looking at things through her eyes for once instead of seeing everything through your own thick skull?"

Beau turned Sassy back toward the cattle and left his words hanging in the air. It ticked Cody off more than he wanted to admit. Mostly because he knew his big brother was right.

Lyssa's next in-home training had been uneventful, not nearly as exciting as her time at the Silverado Ranch. But then, she doubted anything could top the experience she'd had at the ranch. She'd spent three

weeks in Kentucky training a teenage girl to work with
Oscar, a beautiful golden retriever, and she felt confident the two would bond and become a wonderful
team.

She'd thrown herself into her work and managed to
keep her mind off the aching in her heart that never
seemed to go away. During those weeks, the days
moved quickly and the nights slowly. There had been
no dancing, no horse riding. And during the long
nights she found herself missing Cody, his touch, his
warm embrace.

She'd picked up the phone at least ten times during
her stay in Kentucky, intending to call Cody just to
hear his voice. And each time, she replaced the phone
in the cradle before the call could go through. It wasn't
her move. It was Cody's.

The flight back to Houston had been quiet and short,
but still Lyssa felt her feet dragging like the bag she
pulled behind her as she walked through the gate toward the airport terminal.

"What do you mean? I can't leave now. She's just
about to get off the plane."

Her heart leaped forward, colliding against the walls
of her chest. Lyssa knew that voice all too well. She'd
been hearing it in her mind since the moment she
drove away from the Silverado Ranch without Otis.
Without Cody.

"I'm sorry, sir, but dogs aren't allowed in the airport."

People were looking around her, passing her as they
walked off the plane and into the arms of loved ones.
Someone bumped her arm with a piece of luggage as
they tried to get by and she stumbled forward.

Cody had made her feel beautiful in every way by

just being himself. Tears sprang to her eyes. She didn't
think she could bear seeing his eyes when she didn't
live up to the beautiful picture he'd painted of her for
himself.

The officer was standing in front of Cody, hands
like baseball mitts propped on his hips. Otis caught
sight of her and, giving a little yelp of glee, began
wagging his tail. He was seated to Cody's right. And
he didn't have on the proper leash!

Darn it, that man was infuriating. Hadn't Cody listened to one word she'd taught him?

"If you don't leave, I'm going to have to impound
the dog."

Fire seared through Lyssa and quickly turned to
rage.

"This is a guide dog," Cody was saying. "They're
supposed to be allowed in all public places."

"That's right, Officer," Lyssa said, coming up beside him. "Aside from the fact that this gentleman does
not fully appreciate the training that has gone into
making this dog the professional he is, he is indeed a
working dog."

Cody stared at her and her pulse pounded in her
head. He had a black pirate-like patch over one eye.
The other was looking straight at her. The eye she
could see was a mixture of blue and green. She could
finally see it. And it was truly amazing.

She cleared her throat, trying to push her feelings
of longing aside and get to the matter of importance.
"Where's his leash?" she asked Cody harshly.

"I have it with me. I just . . . didn't need it."

"And who are you?" the officer asked Lyssa.

"I'm this dog's trainer." She turned to Cody. "This
airport is like a maze. Why on earth would you . . ."

He was smiling at her, big and bright and goofy and she knew in an instant it was because he could see her. He could *really* see her.

"It worked, Lys."

Tears clung to her eyelashes and blurred her vision. "I know," she whispered, her bottom lip trembling.

"Yeah," he said. He took a step forward but was stopped by the officer's hand.

"You still need to take this dog out of here."

Anger surged through her. "I just told you that Otis is a trained guide dog. He's allowed anywhere his handler is allowed. Mr. Gentry is his handler."

"He may own the dog, but he's not blind."

"How do you know that?"

"Because I'm not blind either. He's been the one leading the dog instead of the other way around. Now either you get a proper leash on him or he's going to be removed."

"I have an extra leash in my bag," Lyssa said.

"Thank you."

The officer stayed while Lyssa rummaged through her suitcase, found the leash, and handed it to Cody. When Cody was through putting it on, the officer walked away.

"Of all the nerve," Lyssa said, her insides burning.

"I know, some people just don't understand the law," Cody said. "I think a strong letter to—"

"No, I mean you! How could you bring Otis in here like this without his proper leash on? Are you trying to ruin my dog!"

"He's my dog. Well, technically my father's dog, but we've sort of come to an agreement on that. Besides, how else would I have known it was you? I couldn't very well go up to everyone coming through the gate and ask if I could sculpt them."

Lyssa started to laugh and just like that, all the anger she wanted to feel evaporated. "That would go over real swell with Officer Know-it-All."

His lips lifted in a sexy grin. "I don't think I'll ever forget the sound of that laugh, though. But just in case, I called the school and talked to your boss. She said you were coming in today. I figured Otis would let me know it was you as soon as he saw you. And he did."

Reaching his hand up to her face, Cody brushed his knuckles across Lyssa's cheek.

"I can't believe I went this long without seeing this," he whispered, his finger stroking her lips.

"Don't do that," she said, stepping back. Her cheeks grew warm and her head became so dizzy she had to catch her breath.

"Why not?"

"Because."

"Oh, now that's a good reason."

Tilting her head to one side, she said, "We're in public."

"So what?"

"People are watching us."

He smiled devilishly. "I don't see anyone watching us. I only see you. And I like very, *very* much what I see."

The trembling of her lip betrayed any kind of control she thought she had. She wanted so much to wrap her arms around Cody and tell him just how much she'd missed him.

"Why did you come here, Cody?"

He sighed. "Because much as I hate to say it, I'm

giving Otis back to the school. You're right. I don't need him now and it wouldn't be fair to deny what he has to give to someone else. And because ... seeing you again is the only thing I've been thinking about since you so rudely left me that Dear John letter on your pillow. Which, by the way, was not a very nice thing to do."

"I wasn't rude. I told you I was leaving."

"And you darned well knew I wasn't going to wait for Dr. Curtis to take off those bandages so you went ahead and left before morning. Just like a coward."

"I am not a coward."

"Thing is, I can't figure out why. I've done nothing but miss you since that day." He swallowed. "I tried to stay away and give you time. I don't know what it is you think you needed or what you hoped I'd figure out, but I'm here to tell you I've been nothing but a bear without you. I think even Otis can't stand me some days."

Lyssa glanced down at Otis, who was obediently sitting next to Cody. On the *wrong* side.

"You're going to ruin my dog if you don't treat him right." She took the leash from Cody's hands and led him to the left side. "Let's get out of here."

As they started to walk, Cody took her suitcase with one hand and draped his other arm around her shoulder. For the first time in weeks, the connection they'd made at the ranch was joined again and Lyssa wondered how she'd survived these last few weeks without him.

"You have a very funny name," Cody said after a time.

"Excuse me?"

"McElhannon. What kind of name is that anyway?"

"Why does this matter?"

"Because names are important. You have to fit your name. I spend a lot of time thinking of the perfect names for my horses."

She stopped walking and glared at him. "So you're comparing me to your horse now?"

"No, I'd never do that. I just don't think Mc-Elhannon suits you."

She propped her hand on her hip. "Oh, really?"

"Now for example, take Gentry. That's a fine name. Easy on the tongue, easy to spell, easy to—"

"I've lived with the name McElhannon all my life and it's suited me just fine, thank you very much. Why are we having this ridiculous conversation in the middle of the airport?"

"I think it's important. I think you should change your name, Lyssa."

She flung her hands in the air with frustration, nerves frayed, her mind jumping between confusion, elation at seeing Cody, and frustration. If Cody didn't kiss her, and quick, she thought she'd lose her mind completely. "And I think you're insane."

He took her by the hand this time and began walking again. Leading her through the crowded airport, ignoring her rant, he went on. "I think Alyssandra Orchid Gentry sounds a lot better than Alyssandra Orchid McElhannon. Yeah, it has a nice ring to it. Don't you think?"

"No, I do not think—" She yanked her hand out of his and stopped short as the words sunk in.

He looked at her, his exposed eye shining so brightly filled with emotion as he gazed at her. "Yeah, Lyssa Gentry. I think that sounds real nice. I could get real used to saying that name."

He dropped the luggage he'd been holding and drew her into his arms before she could utter another idiotic word of protest.

"Why, Cody? I'm nothing like the girls you've dated before."

"I know," he said, smiling. "You're difficult, argumentative, opinionated, stubborn."

"You don't have to keep a running list of my faults. You could at least give me the decency—"

He stifled her protests with a kiss and she seemed to melt in his arms.

"You gentle me, Lyssa," he said quietly when he pulled back to look at her. "I've been a raging engine, spitting out grease and fumes my whole life. But when I'm with you something inside me quiets down. I don't think I can live without that. I don't really want to live without that again."

She opened her mouth to speak but quickly closed it, clamping her teeth over her trembling bottom lip.

He kissed her lightly on the lips, then drew back and stared into her eyes as if he couldn't get his fill. It was there. That same spark of light that she'd envied her sister for. Cody felt it for her. Lyssa knew that without a doubt.

"Tell me what you're so afraid of, Lys."

She looked away. It was like he was looking into her soul when he gazed at her that way.

"I'm not afraid of anything."

"Don't give me that." He came closer, just inches from her and whispered, "I told you you didn't have to lock those fears away from me. They don't matter."

"How can you be sure this is what you really want, Cody? I'm so afraid you're going to wake up one day and find out that none of this is real."

"Marry me. It can't get any more real than that, Lys." He wrapped his strong arms around her waist, picked her up, and spun her around. "Say yes, Lys."

"You're such a fool!" she squealed, suddenly not caring how many people were watching.

Still holding her tight, he threw his head back and laughed. "I've been hearing that a lot lately."

Lyssa laughed as a tear spilled down her cheek. She couldn't remember a time when her heart felt so full she thought it would burst.

"How about we go see about changing that mouthful of a name of yours?"

"You are crazy."

"Crazy in love with you, Lys. Say it. I want to hear you say it."

She hooked her arms around his neck and looked at him as he looked right back at her. Really looked at her with love. "I love you, too, Cody Gentry. Even if you are a crazy fool. And I think Gentry is a beautiful name that I would be proud to share with you."

"You are so very beautiful, Lyssa," he said, brushing the pad of his thumb against her cheek. "But then, I've never needed my eyes to see that."